RIDE A BRIGHT HORSE

RIDE A BRIGHT HORSE

Jennifer Dovey

Matador
9 Priory Business Park,
Wistow Road, Kibworth Beauchamp,
Leicestershire. LE8 0RX
Tel: 0116 279 2299
Email: books@troubador.co.uk
Web: www.troubador.co.uk/matador
Twitter: @matadorbooks

ISBN 978 183859 275 2

British Library Cataloguing in Publication Data.
A catalogue record for this book is available from the British Library.

Printed and bound by CPI Group (UK) Ltd, Croydon, CR0 4YY
Typeset in 10pt Sabon by Troubador Publishing Ltd, Leicester, UK

Matador is an imprint of Troubador Publishing Ltd

To the girls who shared our journey
– Clare, Helen, Jane, Julie, Lindsay, Sally – with my love.

Contents

Acknowledgements

I am sincerely grateful to my husband Trevor for his lovely illustrations, support, encouragement and enthusiasm.

PREFACE

Daisy was my first, last and only horse. She taught me to ride, we were best friends for thirteen years and I was privileged to own her for ten. She always had an opinion and always wanted to be in control, but nevertheless she always looked after me and did her very best to please me in any way she could. She had an uncanny ability to problem-solve, surprising me again and again with her intelligence, good memory and practical common sense. She would nod her head for 'yes' and shake it for 'no', and she could carry out her road drill without being asked to 'look right, left and right again' – to the amusement of many a passer-by.

Her memory was also excellent. My favourite route took us to a crossroads, and I could say,

"When we get to the bottom of the hill, turn left," and she would do so without any further prompting, either physical or verbal. We must have hacked thousands and thousands of miles, and in our heyday we were riding for three or four hours several times a week. Friends used to say to me, "I worry about you, miles away from home, all on your own in the middle of no-where for hours," and I would say, "I'm not on my own, I'm with Daisy."

Going for long walks in hand became part of our lives as well, on days when it was too cold or too hot to ride. I spent many happy hours strolling with my friend in hand, high up on the Downs, watching the racehorses exercise, soaking up the sunshine, drinking in the view, listening to the birdsong. I could have made a journey of a thousand miles with her and there would not have been anything we could possibly encounter on the way which we could not have dealt with as a team, either in hand or under saddle. No matter what the obstacle – quick-sand, bogs, stampeding cattle, snarling angry dogs, lost sheep, roadblocks, pneumatic drills, accidents, ambulances, motorway bridges, heavy traffic, floods, or even the most extreme weather the countryside could throw at us – she never let me down or left me behind.

I remember so well the first day we met, the early days when I was learning to ride and my nervousness, when we rode out for the very first time, all on our own! We were always a team right from the start, and long before she became mine everyone called her 'Jen's Daisy'.

So many memories, so much love, so much mischief, so many times she saved the day, made me laugh or made me feel humbled. My greatest joy was to have known her and to have been her friend for so many years, and her gift to me was to set me free.

CHAPTER ONE

DAISY

Daisy was doing what she liked best, mooching around in the long grass, collecting bright golden dandelions. She loved the fact that the cheerful little flower heads had so many tiny petals and that they seemed to glow so brightly against the thick emerald green grass. The warm sun shone down on her back as she pottered about, foraging happily. The white farmhouse at the end of the lane gleamed in the sunlight against a perfectly clear, bright blue sky, and the warm breeze smelled deliciously of fragrant grasses and flowers.

It was a perfect day. Daisy felt really quite sleepy with contentment and closed her eyes for a moment, basking in the warmth from the sun.

"Daisy! Daisy!"

She opened her eyes and saw Tina coming along the lane towards the gate, a bright red head collar in her hand.

"Come on, Daisy!" called Tina "It's time to do some work."

Daisy sauntered amiably towards the gate to meet Tina, whom she liked very much. Tina had not worked at the riding stable for very long but all the horses seemed to like her quiet and gentle manner, both on the ground and in the saddle. She deftly slid the head collar over Daisy's soft black velvet ears and clipped the lead rope underneath her chin. Daisy yawned.

"Gosh, Daisy, you've been eating dandelions again – your tongue is all yellow," said Tina, grinning. She patted Daisy's neck and slid her hand up to the thick black and white mane, running her fingers through the tangle.

"Come on, girly." she said. "We have to get you cleaned up for a hack, and that mane is going to take some work for a start. It's a new lady; her name is Jenny. She's learning to ride and is very nervous, so you have to be very, *very* good today. No mischief!"

To be fair, it was not often that Daisy was anything else *but* very, very good. She was not a big horse – technically she was a pony because of the height of her withers – and most of her work for the riding school was to teach teenagers and small adults. Daisy liked the teenagers best because, usually, they could already ride quite well. Most of them were keen to gallop about – when they were not supposed to – and often they were learning to jump as well. Fortunately, galloping about and jumping were Daisy's second and third favourite things after eating dandelions. Neither the children nor the teenagers felt heavy on Daisy's back and she enjoyed their noisy chatter and laughter. The only downside was that they invariably had lessons, these being usually 'in school', and Daisy much preferred to be out in the open and on the hills, cantering upon the soft downland grass under a big blue sky, with a warm breeze blowing through her mane. The bigger horses tended to go out on hacks more often because adults from the city came to ride at weekends; and at weekends the yard teemed with children having lessons. Consequently, opportunities to be used to hack out were quite rare in Daisy's life, and the chance of a ride over the hills on such a gloriously sunny day as this was a real treat!

So, whilst it was true to say that Daisy was ordinarily very, very good… Well, there were the odd occasions, when being out on the downs was *so* good that Daisy just couldn't resist taking off with her rider and cantering freely, her mane flying in the wind, her long thick white tail streaming out behind her, hooves featherlight on the thick green turf.

Such a pleasure, such a feeling of freedom, such a joy to be alive. Such behaviour, however, did not go down well with the escorts who were taking the rides, as it was their job to keep all the clients safe. If a client fell off, or was frightened because their horse misbehaved, it was not good for the reputation of the school. Of course, Daisy was not stupid and she knew better than anyone else the ability of her rider, since it was she who was being ridden! Quite often, as she well knew, the rider on those occasions was perfectly happy with Daisy's mischief, and some of the teenagers actually encouraged it and egged her on.

Tina had thought about all of this. She knew Daisy very well and had ridden her more than most of the staff as she herself was quite slim and slightly built. She loved the fact that Daisy was spirited and full of fun, loved her athleticism and graceful movement, and fully appreciated her unfailing enthusiasm for everything.

Somewhere in Daisy's ancestry there must have been a finely built racehorse or a thoroughbred or two as, although Daisy had the look of a light piebald cob, with thick hair, sturdy bottom, strong back and big feet, she was at the same time light on her feet and very nimble. Best of all, she was very fast. When the staff played games of 'Chase me Charlie' after their own training sessions, or when there were jumping competitions against the clock, Tina knew that she and Daisy would be a winning combination.

Above all else, she trusted Daisy and was confident that the route she had chosen for this morning's hack gave no opportunity for unplanned cantering off. In addition, for her own mount she had chosen a horse which was one of her favourites for use as a lead horse, a paddock chum of Daisy's. Missy was probably about the same age as Daisy, perhaps a little older, slightly bigger, but she had a much more obedient temperament and was often chosen for adult novices as her pace was even and fairly slow. Tina knew that Missy would neither canter off nor want to rush about, and that Daisy would be delighted to partner her old friend as they so seldom worked together. Even better, it was the time of year when all the horses lived out all night, and this more natural existence, coupled with the sweet summer grass, calmed them all down a great deal. At other times of year, sharp frosts, windy weather and being in their stables at night sometimes caused a build-up of unspent energy, resulting in frisky eagerness under saddle and high jinks in the paddock.

Tina hummed to herself as she finished tacking up both the mares. She glanced at her watch; it was 10:45 a.m. She had time for a quick cup of coffee before meeting her new client at 11 a.m.

Chapter Two

Jenny

For the umpteenth time, Jenny looked at her watch nervously. She had been at the yard for almost an hour, wandering around and soaking up the atmosphere, patting the horses which had their heads over their stable doors. *They certainly all seem friendly enough*, she thought. The riding school was well known locally for the quality of its horses, and Jenny had heard that there were strict rules about how many hours a week the horses worked, so that they had plenty of time to rest, graze and just enjoy being horses with their friends in the paddocks. The school was situated at the foot of some beautiful downland, and the highest hill in the county was nearby. It was a perfect place to hack out around the countryside, and the horses benefitted from an ideal mix of exercise which kept them all strong and fit and happy in their work.

Jenny had not been riding for very long. She could just about mount, dismount, walk and trot happily enough but her quite exceptional nervousness had prevented her from making progress. She found the lessons in the school quite terrifying. She could not really say why, but for one thing it seemed unnatural to her to be riding around in circles and, for another, the grey metal walls of the indoor school seemed to come towards her at an alarming speed when she was riding at a trot – she felt as if she would crash. The horses all seemed good-natured enough, but she did not ride the same ones often enough to really get a feel for their characters and, as she knew so little about them, she found it almost impossible to really trust them.

Her instructor, Sue, had realised that there was absolutely no possibility of Jenny trying to learn to canter in the school and had suggested that she take advantage of the time of year to begin to hack out around the countryside. Sue hoped that Jenny would relax whilst riding out at a leisurely pace in the sunshine and that, gradually, she might gain enough confidence to try a little canter out of doors. Jenny was fairly small – not quite as slim as Tina, about 10 cm shorter. Sue had discussed with Tina which horse might be the most suitable to be used every week for Jenny's hack, and together they had decided upon Daisy. If she seemed to be in a mischievous mood beforehand, well, Tina would be able to give her a little canter in school before the hack, just to get rid of some surplus energy.

Jenny could hear her heart thumping loudly as she climbed the steps to the office at exactly 10:55 a.m. Tina was already there and recognised her at once, coming forward to shake her hand warmly.

"It's a wonderful day for a hack," she said, smiling broadly. "How are you feeling?"

"Terrified," replied Jenny with a rueful smile, "but I often feel like this before a lesson as well. I can't explain it and I just don't know what to do about it."

"Then a stroll in the sunshine is just what you need," said Tina. "Off we go, then. Best not to keep the ladies waiting."

To Jenny's surprise, the 'ladies', Missy and Daisy, were in adjoining stalls, both with their heads over their respective stable doors, both dozing, with eyes closed and their lower lips hanging open. Tina giggled.

"They're not exactly on fire with enthusiasm, are they?" she asked as she opened Daisy's door, stroked her under the chin to rouse her and led her along to the old stone mounting block.

Jenny agreed and thought to herself, *Maybe this is going to be OK!*

She was very keen to try riding out of the indoor school and into the countryside as Sue had suggested. She had always loved the countryside and had always had dogs, so being out of doors in all wind and weather seemed entirely normal to her and much more like 'her territory' than the indoor school.

Daisy, now wide awake and attentive, stood politely and patiently while Tina helped Jenny onto her saddle and made sure she was safe and comfortable before leading Missy out of her stable and nimbly hopping on.

"Off we go," she said cheerily, and nudged Missy into walk, before lifting each leg in turn and tightening her own girth on both sides. It made Jenny feel ill just to watch. She was almost too frightened to move a muscle; but as they made their way out of the yard and rode under the cool pale green canopy of the lime trees towards the track, she began to relax. Daisy blew down her nose and nodded her head.

"That's a good sign," said Tina. "It's 'chill out' time, Daisy!"

Daisy fell into step alongside Missy as the two mares joined the white chalk track. The strong sun shone down upon it, emphasising the brilliant whiteness of its bleached stones in dramatic contrast to the thick green grass on either side. The rolling hills in the distance were dotted with tiny figures of seemingly immobile sheep; from far away the paler grass looked soft and inviting against the cloudless blue sky.

The track began to rise more steeply as they headed uphill and altered course to the left, and before long they were joined by quite a stiff breeze. Tina chattered away and occasionally answered her mobile phone, which Jenny found quite unnerving. How you could text messages with one hand, while holding your reins with the other, and ride a horse without even looking where you were going, all at the same time? She hadn't a clue. Tina was clearly a very accomplished rider. Tina turned to look at her.

"You are allowed to breathe, you know. You're as still as a statue!"

"I'm concentrating," Jenny replied. "Heels down, sit tall, elbows in, shoulders back, soft knees, gently allow the reins to move forward in your hands with each pace – there is so much to remember all at once."

"Well, it will all come naturally very soon," said Tina reassuringly. "The beauty of hacking is that you cannot help but relax in such peaceful surroundings. A relaxed rider makes for a relaxed horse, and a relaxed horse is easier to ride, always remember that."

Tina had stopped at a small gate whilst she was talking and she leaned over to open it to allow Daisy and Jenny to go through.

"Immediately you are in the field, turn Daisy to face the gate, Jenny; that way she is not likely to suddenly scamper off with you up the hill," Tina advised.

"Do you think she would do that?" asked Jenny in alarm.

"Well, not today perhaps," said Tina with a grin; "she looks very chilled out to me, so she obviously feels very comfortable with you on board. You must have a good seat!"

Jenny wasn't too sure what that meant but it sounded encouraging so she grinned back.

Tina followed Jenny through the gate, closed it with a shove of her foot and waited while Jenny turned Daisy around so that the gate was behind them. They set off again at a walk. There was no track in this field, but they picked their way up a tiny path which the sheep had trodden over time, and loose stones clattered back down the hill behind them as they progressed. They were climbing higher now and, as they rounded the side of the hill and turned west, the sky began to cloud over and the breeze became even stronger. They had to walk in single file because the trail was so narrow and, as Missy was a little bigger than Daisy with longer legs and a longer stride, she and Tina were getting further ahead. Jenny was afraid to give Daisy a little nudge or a kick in case Daisy misinterpreted her signal and took it as an invitation to trot – or, even worse, go faster! So she sat quietly and hoped that before long they would stop climbing and she would be able to catch up. To the left of them was another field full of sheep, their bedraggled woolly coats hanging off them in grubby clumps. There was a fence between the two fields and some large bushes dotted around; *useful windbreaks if you are a sheep*, thought Jenny as the breeze played around with Daisy's mane and blew her forelock back over her ears.

Whilst they had been walking, Jenny had noticed that Daisy often looked to her left – and suddenly Daisy stopped. She looked to her left again, this time mouthing her bit as she stared at the sheep over the fence.

"Come on, Daisy," said Jenny, "we are falling further and further behind."

Cautiously, she gave Daisy a little nudge with her foot and, to her horror, Daisy actually turned to the left this time and headed for the fence!

"Tina!" she called. "Tina!" but her voice blew back at her on the breeze and Tina didn't turn around. Daisy ambled on, quickening her pace a little, and Jenny desperately tried to remember what to do. She pulled the reins back towards her but it made no difference whatsoever. In her mind she could hear Sue saying, '*Use your voice, Jenny, your voice is one of your seven aids.*'

"Stop, Daisy, stop!" she cried, with what she hoped sounded more like authority than desperation. She pulled the reins back towards her again, as hard as she possibly could, and leaned back at the same time, but Daisy simply ignored her. *How absurd is it to be talking to a horse?* she thought – *how are we to know if they understand the language of a human? This one clearly doesn't!* Daisy reached the fence and stopped for a moment, sniffed at the large bush to the right of them then looked out over the fence at the sheep with their heads down. Jenny could feel the panic rising within her. What was Daisy thinking of? she wondered; she wouldn't jump the fence, would she?

"Oh help, please, please don't jump the fence, Daisy!" she cried in desperation.

At that, to Jenny's immense relief, Daisy began to turn around; but having turned a full 360 degrees she stopped again, looked left up the hill in the direction of Missy and Tina, and promptly began to walk backwards. *Oh goodness,* thought Jenny, *what on earth is she going to do now?* She could feel tears welling up behind her eyes and, not for the first time, wondered if she was really cut out to be a rider. What was the use of learning to give signals if the horse just ignored them?!

"Tina!" she yelled again. "Tina! Help!"

Daisy lifted each hind hoof, placed it down again slightly away from her body and stood quite still.

Jenny started to say, "Come on, Daisy, good girl, please, let's go and join Missy—" when she heard a noise like water gushing and she looked down – Daisy was having a pee!

Tina and Missy re-appeared at that moment.

"What on earth are you doing hiding behind a bush?" asked Tina. "I suddenly realised you weren't there and I couldn't see you anywhere – are you OK? What's going on?"

"She wouldn't listen to me," said Jenny, "she kept looking to the left, and then all of a sudden she came over here and I couldn't stop her, then she turned around, backed up against the fence at the side of this big bush and went for a pee."

Tina roared with laughter. "What a practical girl you are, Daisy!"

"Why did she hide? Didn't she want anyone to see her pee?" asked Jenny, bemused.

"Oh, it wasn't that," said Tina; "it's windy, and she didn't want to get her legs splashed, that's all. She's probably been looking for a big enough bush for the last half hour."

Jenny stared at Tina in a mixture of amazement and disbelief. She looked down at Daisy and back at Tina who, still chuckling, was turning Missy round and heading back up the hill. Jenny followed them and, once they were on the spine of the hill, the clouds started to clear and the sun came out again. Within a few minutes the strong breeze had quietened to a whisper and Jenny could feel the warmth of the sun on her back again. They stopped once or twice for Tina to point out landmarks in the distance, the tall spire of the village church towering over a row of old cottages alongside it, and the woods on the other side of the village which Tina promised would deliver plenty of lovely hacks in the future.

As they retraced their steps down the long chalk track back to the yard, Jenny began to feel much more comfortable and, she decided, safer. For one thing, the challenging part of the ride was now over and she could see the yard in the distance; they would soon be home and she would have her first hack 'under her belt'. For another, the horses had dropped their heads a little and walked comfortably side by side, blowing down their noses from time to time, clearly relaxed. Tina let her reins dangle and just held on to the buckle, letting Missy stretch her neck right down to the floor before lifting her head again to a normal height.

Jenny rode along lost in thought, mulling over the incident on the hill. *How funny*, she thought. *Here I am, nervously expecting this big, unpredictable animal beneath me to take off with me at a gallop at any moment, jump a fence without warning, throw me off, do... well, heaven knows what else. I hadn't really thought about what she might be thinking, or even if she thinks anything at all. And meanwhile, here is Daisy, desperate to have a pee, not wanting to do so in the wind, and the only thought in her head is where to find a big enough bush to shelter behind to keep her legs clean and dry. Simply amazing!*

She was still thinking about it after they had untacked the horses. While Tina brushed them off, cleaned their feet and put them back in their stables, Jenny took the tack back to the tack room, then returned and stood by Daisy's stable door and watched her for a while. Tina had put a large pile of hay in one corner of the stable, and Daisy was pulling mouthfuls of it from the pile and moving them around. She had put little piles all along one side of the stable and around the corner, and was placing them neatly along the other side when she realised Jenny was looking at her. She nickered in recognition and came over to the door.

"There's more to you than meets the eye, Daisy May," Jenny said thoughtfully as she stroked Daisy's long white nose with the backs of her fingers. Daisy stretched her head forward over the door and Jenny stood still like a statue, not daring to move as Daisy sniffed the front of her jacket and nuzzled all around her throat and to the side of her neck, her warm breath blowing softly on Jenny's skin.

"I think you've made a friend," said Tina as she came around the corner, a hay net in each hand.

"Do you really think she likes me?" asked Jenny.

"Well," replied Tina, "there's only one way to find out, isn't there? Shall I book you in for the same time next week?"

Jenny nodded, gave Daisy a final stroke and turned to go home for her own tea. She gave her neck a little rub; she could still feel the warmth of Daisy's breath upon it, and she felt quite emotional about Daisy's apparent display of affection and friendship towards her. She was used to dogs and had grown up in their company, but knew nothing about horses. However, she had learned more from Daisy in one afternoon than she had from all the other horses she had ridden in school over the past few months. Was hacking out the key to success? she wondered. Did being in an entirely natural environment allow the horses more freedom to display their natural characteristics? And if so, was it more difficult to control them out there on the hills? She hoped that the latter was not true but was eager to know more and could hardly wait until the next ride.

CHAPTER THREE

THE FIRST CANTER

The following Thursday, Jenny arrived at the yard an hour before her ride, as usual. She usually found that wandering around for an hour, watching the horses in the paddocks and patting them in their stables, was a much better way of forgetting her nerves than arriving at the last minute and feeling rushed. She loved the bustle – girls with barrows, girls with hay nets, the sound of shod hooves clattering on the old cobbles. There were always dogs running around, and often they would find brushes or other items around the stables and run off with them, noisily playing tug-of-war with any other dog which wanted to join in. She was just considering whether she had enough time for a cup of hot chocolate from the vending machine in the office when Tina came around the corner.

"Ah, there you are," she said. "I was looking for you. I finished my other hack a little early today and Daisy is all ready for you. Shall we go?"

They walked together to Daisy's stable where she was standing patiently with her head hanging over the door, looking in their direction.

"I used her as an escort today," said Tina. "It's good practice for her to be in charge for a change instead of following. And it means that she's not as fresh as she was at 10 a.m., so that's nice for you to know! I think it's a perfect opportunity for you to try your first little canter today, if you feel up to it when we get there."

Jenny felt her stomach turn over with fear.

"Well, I don't know…" She trailed off, not wanting to sound 'wet' but not really knowing what else to say.

"I think you'll be surprised," said Tina. "Trust me."

She had been leading Daisy out of her stable towards the mounting block as she spoke and, whilst Tina held onto Daisy, Jenny climbed the steps and went through the process she had been taught to check everything prior to mounting. Satisfied, she placed her left foot in the stirrup, swung her other leg over Daisy's rump with ease and landed very softly in the saddle. Once she had collected up her reins, Tina let go of Daisy and hopped onto Missy from the ground.

"Ready?" she asked, going through her usual routine of lifting her legs high in the air while tightening her girth.

Jenny nodded and took a deep breath as they made their way out of the yard.

They started their ride on the same chalk track as the last time but, instead of altering course to climb the hill, they kept straight on. The track was straight and flat for some distance beyond them and they had not gone very far before Tina said, "Right, lesson time. Watch what I do." And she lifted her bottom out of her saddle and leaned forward very slightly.

"Do you see my position, Jenny? Heels right down; your weight is in your heels. Bottom lifted and very slightly behind its usual saddle position. Have you seen jockeys ride a bit like this? We call it half-seat." Jenny nodded. "And do you see the extra leather strap over Daisy's neck today? Well, when I say so, take the strap in both hands and rest your fingers on Daisy's neck for support, keep hold of your reins just as they are, keep your heels down and lift your bottom a little off your saddle. We are just walking, don't worry about a thing; we are going to stay in walk until you get the hang of this new position."

Jenny found it quite a bit to remember but she went through the various movements and after a few tries, when she wobbled a bit and had to sit down again, she discovered that there was one particular position where both her feet and her bottom were in the perfect place and she found it quite easy to balance.

"Lift your chin a little so that you can look where you are going," said Tina.

"Perfect, Jenny, perfect. OK, sit back in the saddle again and I will count to ten; when I get to ten, get into your new position again. One, two three…"

Jenny practised again and again. Tina gave her some 'fine-tuning' instructions as they walked along in a straight line and, after a while, Jenny began to feel quite confident.

"Fantastic!" beamed Tina. "You have grasped that much more quickly than some people do. OK, now for the next part of the lesson."

They had reached a fork in the track and to the right was an old wooden gate. Tina flipped the latch and went through it, reminding Jenny as she did so to turn and face the gate immediately she was inside. To their right, was a long 'V' shape cut in the hill; it looked as if an ancient stream or river, now dry, had cut its way through the chalk over thousands of years. The 'V' shape was quite narrow, not much more than the width of a horse with rider, and it rose at a gentle gradient. Jenny could see the end of it in the distance where it finished by some young trees at the top of the hill.

"Now, then," said Tina, "this is the plan. I am going to lead, and Daisy will follow Missy. I am going to control the speed so Daisy can't go too fast; she can't overtake as there is not enough room. We are going to walk, then trot, and I am going to count to three. When I say three, get into sitting trot and, as soon as you feel confident, rise into your new 'jockey' position and hold onto the strap as I showed you. If you feel wobbly, sit down again and then get up as soon as you feel able. If you feel yourself tipping forward, push against Daisy's neck to right yourself. Any problems, just shout 'stop' and I will slow down to a walk. OK? Any questions?"

Jenny thought through the sequence which Tina had described. She could see that starting, speed, distance, finishing, wobbling and the danger of Daisy taking off with her had been covered in Tina's plan, and in spite of her nervousness she was keen to try.

"I'm ready!" she replied, with a bit more confidence than she actually felt.

Tina nudged Missy into a walk and, while looking back over her shoulder at Jenny almost the whole time, they increased their pace to trot, then Tina said, "OK, one, two, three…"

Jenny got into the half-seat position almost immediately – she was surprised how bouncy the canter was and held on grimly to Daisy's neck strap, pushing against Daisy's neck to keep herself upright. Her thighs started to ache and her bottom touched the saddle briefly before she pulled herself up again. Tina began to slow down and, within seconds, they were at the top.

"Wow!" exclaimed Jenny. "Wow! I did it! I did it!"

"You certainly did," said Tina, smiling broadly. "Well done, lass. Give Daisy a pat and tell her she's a good girl too."

They walked on a little way past the small clump of trees at the top and negotiated another small gate at the top on the left. It led back onto the same wide chalk track they had started out on, and Tina once again dropped her reins so that Missy could stretch her neck on the way home. Jenny felt exhilarated and, at the same time, almost tearful with the emotion of success.

"I can't wait to do that again!" she said excitedly.

"Well, I'm glad about that," replied Tina, "having seen how well you did. I have a suggestion to make to you. Do you know Billie at the yard?"

Jenny shook her head. She had seen Billie several times, a tall girl in her twenties with thick red hair and a loud voice, but she had not been introduced to her and their paths had never crossed.

"Billie is a friend of mine," said Tina. "She takes a group hack on a Saturday morning, novices like yourself, a few capable children and some teenagers as well; they are all just learning to canter in school, and Billie usually starts them off out of doors, exactly where we have just been – The Cutting, we call it. Would you like to join them?"

"Are you sure I'm good enough?" asked Jenny. Even though they had only hacked out a couple of times, she liked Tina's ways and really felt that Tina understood how nervous she was. Maybe someone else might not be as patient.

"Absolutely sure, and I promise I will tell Billie all about you too. A week is a long time between practices when you are learning, so if you could ride twice a week through the summer, I am sure you will make excellent progress."

Jenny thought about this last comment; it was true that a week seemed an eternity sometimes. Although she had had difficulties with her confidence, she loved the horses and the atmosphere around the yard, and she desperately wanted to ride more competently and as soon as possible. Perhaps this was an ideal solution.

"OK," she said. "I'll have a go."

Chapter Four

Billie

Saturday morning dawned bright and clear. Jenny was pleased; she had not yet had to ride in the rain, having only been in the school for a short time, and had no idea what it would be like, or whether the horses behaved any differently in wet weather. Today would bring enough challenges without bad weather, she thought – an escort she had not met, other horses and riders she did not know, and Tina would not be there to reassure her. On the positive side, she had been assured that the ride would be the same one Tina had used for her first canter, so at least that would be familiar and she knew what to expect. She was also riding Daisy again and looking forward very much to doing so.

When she arrived at the yard she was amazed at the sheer volume of people. Parents who had brought their children for their Saturday lessons had also brought their younger siblings, some of them in pushchairs, and there were more dogs than Jenny had ever seen before too. The stables were largely empty; some of the occupants were tacked up and tied up outside their stable doors waiting to be untacked, groomed and put away with some hay before their next lesson. Girls leading ponies, both with and without riders, were everywhere. Some of the larger horses which had finished their work were being washed off and led out to their paddocks.

Wilhelmina Frobisher – also known as Billie – was coming out of the tack room with a saddle under each arm when she noticed Jenny.

"Good morning!" she boomed. "Running late, I'm afraid. Can you give me a hand, Jenny?"

"With pleasure," replied Jenny, "but you will have to tell me what to do, I'm afraid."

"No problem," said Billie. "Hold this." And she handed Jenny one of the saddles with a saddlecloth underneath and a bridle and girth draped over it.

"Back in a mo," she said, before disappearing into the tack room again and returning with two more saddles. "This way, Jenny."

Jenny followed her to a long run of stables which ran at right angles to the main yard. There were four ponies left in the run, and Billie placed a saddle over each of the four stable doors. Three of the ponies were smaller than Daisy and one was about the same size, Jenny noted.

"Are they all coming out with us?" asked Jenny.

"Yes," replied Billie, "seven of us this morning – these four, I'm riding Cara, you have Daisy and Olly is being ridden in school; he will be finished in a minute and at least he's tacked up. If you go and wait by the mounting block, I'll be with you in a minute."

Jenny did as she was asked, and Billie arrived with two ponies on lead ropes, one in each hand, and proceeded to pass them to four Saturday girls, who helped the ponies' riders to mount and made sure the girths were tight enough. Olly came out of the school with his rider already seated, a boy of about fourteen called Ed, and Tina arrived with Daisy whilst Billie went off to get Cara, her own bay mare of about 16 hands.

"I thought I would come and see you off," said Tina, holding onto Daisy whilst Jenny mounted. Jenny leaned forward and gave Daisy a pat. She was so pleased to see her again so soon and was feeling, all things considered, remarkably relaxed.

Once they were all assembled, Billie headed out of the yard with Cara, the others trailing behind in single file. Daisy was the last but one in line, with Olly and Ed bringing up the rear. This time, they turned right instead of joining the chalk track, and made their way through the little village street, past the church and the row of old cottages. One or two people were busy cutting their lawns in the small cottage gardens and they stopped their mowers to wave as the string of horses passed by. As the group neared the crossroads, Jenny became aware of a strong acrid smell of burning and could hear the sound of a loud generator or motor.

The sound of men's voices shouting above the din grew louder as they approached. The road was not very wide, and on one side was a large lorry, its trailer tipped, unloading tarmac, and there were three men spreading the tarmac around with shovels. The stench was terrible and there was a cacophony of noise. The fumes made Jenny's eyes water and Daisy shook her head once or twice as if she did not like the noise, or the smell either. Probably both, thought Jenny. To the right of the lorry was just enough room for two horses with riders to pass; and Billie had led the ride to about halfway along the side of the lorry, when Cara's front legs lifted up off the ground and she began to skitter backwards.

"Go on, girl," shouted Billie, "get on!" Cara took two steps forward before balking at the road workers again, and this time she tried to spin to the right to head back in the direction of the yard. "Stop it, will you!" bellowed Billie. "Cara! Walk on, walk on!" She hit Cara on the rump with her riding crop and tried to urge her forwards and past the lorry again. Cara was rooted to the spot, then her front feet started to lift simultaneously as if she were about to rear, and the ponies in the line began to fidget. Jenny sat very still, watching anxiously.

Daisy had not yet moved a muscle, but now she stepped to the right at a walking pace and overtook the first pony, then the second, seemingly oblivious to the lorry, the men, the smell and the noise. When she was almost level with Cara, she nodded her head towards her and slowed down as she overtook her. Then she nodded towards Cara a second time before looking straight ahead again. Cara calmed and followed Daisy instantly, and the ponies walked behind them in an orderly line. A few metres further on, when they were clear of the lorry, Billie and Cara came alongside and Daisy promptly dropped behind them to allow Cara to take the lead once more.

Jenny was simply amazed. Daisy's actions had been entirely of her own volition, she herself had played absolutely no part in taking control of the situation, but what would Billie think? Would she think Jenny was trying to show off? Was it usual, wondered Jenny, for a horse to take control of a difficult situation like that? She made a mental note to ask Tina about it. She leaned forward and gave Daisy a well-deserved pat.

"Clever girl," she whispered.

Billie led the ride through the village, across the road and around the base of the hill until they reached the first gate at the bottom of The Cutting. After giving everyone instructions on what to do – as Tina had done with Jenny two days earlier – she opened the gate and the ponies filed in and turned around to face the gate. Whilst they had been walking to The Cutting, Jenny had been repeating the instructions for her canter position over and over again in her head and, when Billie lined them up to start their walk and then increased the pace first to trot, then to canter, Jenny knew exactly what to do. The canter felt a little faster and a little smoother than the first time, and by the time they reached the top Jenny was grinning from ear to ear. Billie had been glancing back at them now and then as they followed her, just to ensure they were all safe, and once everyone was at the top she gave a hearty "Hurrah! Well done, chaps!" and congratulated them all on a job well done. As they filed down the chalk track back to the yard, Jenny thought how wonderful it must be to have your own horse like Billie did and to be able to ride like this on any day you pleased.

Chapter Five

Jenny Falls Off

Over the next few days, Jenny thought about Daisy a lot. She was very proud of what she had done when Cara was too frightened to go past the roadworks. It appeared to Jenny that Daisy had some problem-solving ability and she wondered whether this was normal for all horses, or was Daisy just a little bit special? She herself was certainly becoming rather attached to Daisy and, on the following Thursday when Jenny arrived at the yard, instead of wandering around the stables, she went to see Daisy first. Daisy had her head

down in her stable, munching away on the little piles of hay which she had spread around the sides of her stable. She nickered in recognition when she saw Jenny and came over to the door for a pat.

"Hello, gorgeous," said Jenny, rubbing her behind one soft black velvet ear. "I wonder what Tina has in store for us today?"

Tina was in the office finishing a cup of coffee and looked up and smiled as Jenny came through the door.

"How was your group hack on Saturday?" she asked. "Did you enjoy it?"

"It was great," said Jenny enthusiastically; "my second canter was easier than my first and it felt a bit smoother too. Did Billie mention the roadworks to you?"

"Mmm, yes," said Tina. "I gather you saved the day?"

"Well, *I* didn't exactly," replied Jenny, "I didn't do anything at all, it was Daisy, not me, and I was worried that Billie might have thought I was showing off or something."

"She didn't think that, no," said Tina thoughtfully, "but she was rather surprised that you took charge of the situation. Did you really not have anything to do with it at all?"

"No, honestly, I didn't," said Jenny. "I was going to ask you whether it was usual for horses to take charge like that and take over as leader?"

"Well, to be honest, no," replied Tina. "It's the sort of thing a mare which is used to leading might do, if she has been in charge of a herd for example, but they are usually older and more experienced horses. I wonder if young

Daisy is not as young as we first thought. Well, back to today," she said, briskly moving on.

"How do you feel about two little canters? We can practise your position on the way, as we did last week, and we can then have a first canter at The Cutting, which will be your third time.

"Then, if I'm happy that you can balance well, there is a grassy strip on top of the hill which is straight and flat – we call it The Little Gallop, but don't let that put you off. We use it for people learning to canter as it is a nice length, not too long. There is a fence at the end of it, and all the riding school horses know that we pull up as we approach the fence. Daisy may not have been there very often, she may not have been there at all in fact, but I am riding Missy again and I will control the pace. What do you think? "

Jenny nodded eagerly. The idea of two canters sounded like double the pleasure and, for once, she did not feel quite as nervous.

Within the hour they were at the wooden gate leading onto The Cutting again. Tina had been very pleased with Jenny's balance in her practices on the way there, and Jenny felt that her thighs were getting stronger as they did not ache quite so much. Their first canter seemed to Jenny to pass very quickly, and this time she was able to keep in position the whole time without her bottom touching the saddle.

Tina looked back at Jenny, smiling broadly, and said with a grin, "Well, no need to ask how that felt! Now then, this next canter is entirely flat so it is important not to lean too far forward. Remember, your weight is in your heels."

Tina rose out of her saddle into the jockey position.

"Look at my position; you can imagine a straight vertical line running from my heels upwards, and my bottom is very slightly behind the vertical line – look what happens when I lean too far forward."

Jenny could see how the centre of balance was firmly set when Tina was in the right place but it looked as if she would topple forward any minute when she leaned too far forward over Missy's neck.

"Yes, I see," she answered

"OK," said Tina, "the usual format, we go through the gate, turn to face it and we both turn away at the same time. We commence in walk, then transition to trot, sitting trot, then canter. One final thing: it isn't a very long canter but it might feel faster as it's flat. Your balance looks good, but if you feel panicky just take a deep breath, hold your strap and concentrate on holding your position; or if you are really worried, just shout 'Stop!' and we will slow down."

Jenny nodded, feeling quite excited.

They walked on and, as they went through the gate onto The Little Gallop, Jenny's first thought was what a long way off the fence seemed, and she felt the familiar little lurch in her tummy.

"OK?" enquired Tina, seeing her serious expression.

"Yes, I think so," replied Jenny as they turned at the same time to face up the strip towards the fence line.

"Off we go, then," said Tina. "Walk… trot… sit… Ready? Canter!"

As Daisy changed her pace, Jenny rose up out of the saddle, checking her balance as she did so and running through all the various elements of her position in her mind: heels down, bottom a little back, head up, hold onto the neck strap; she suddenly realised how fast they were going and how smooth the ground felt beneath them, yet soft, and almost springy like a mattress. She felt a little thrill of excitement and almost forgot that Tina and Missy were there; she was only conscious of her own body and Daisy's rhythmic movement beneath her, as if they were contained in their own little fast-moving bubble, totally disconnected from the rest of the world.

They were halfway to the fence when Jenny heard a roar behind her and out of the corner of her right eye, almost parallel with them, she saw a huge hot-air balloon rising from the valley below them. Simultaneously, Daisy seemed to throw all her legs to one side and back again whilst keeping her body straight, and the tiny jolt, coupled with the sudden distraction of the balloon, took Jenny by surprise and caused her to lose her balance. She started to tip to the left, and the next thing she knew she floated to the ground very gently as if someone had caught her and lowered her onto the thick soft grass. Daisy stopped instantly and stood like a statue, motionless, staring straight ahead at the fence. At the same time, Tina threw them a backward glance and her eyes widened in horror as she saw Jenny on the ground. She quickly turned Missy around and came back at a trot.

"Oh my goodness, are you OK?" she asked anxiously.

"Perfectly OK, thank you," said Jenny. "That was weird. I fell so slowly it was almost as if someone caught me and gently put me on the ground. I don't even remember taking my feet out of the stirrups, it all happened so fast."

"Just look at Daisy!" exclaimed Tina. "I can't believe she stopped and waited for you! She must really, really like you! Normally in these situations mischievous horses like Daisy are off and away and we have to go after them and catch them. Yet here she is, on the softest, longest, good canter ground she has seen for ages with a really scary monster balloon right next to her and she's waiting for you. I just can't believe it!"

Tina took hold of Daisy's reins, rubbing her on the neck and praising her as she did so, whilst Jenny got up and dusted herself down. She did not feel bruised or injured in any way, just a little shocked and a bit shaky too.

"Up you get," said Tina. "Can you mount from the ground or shall I get off and give you a leg-up?"

"I'll have a go," replied Jenny, and after a few attempts she managed it.

"I think we'll just trot up to the fence, just in case," said Tina. "That's enough excitement for one day."

They were not far from the fence line and arrived there without further mishap and walked around the outside edge of the field back to the little gate where they had come in.

Jenny found that the shakiness she felt soon passed as they enjoyed a relaxing walk back down the track to the yard, chatting all the way. After they had untacked the horses and brushed them down Tina said, "They are both going out into the same paddock now as they both have the rest of the day off. Do you want to help me turn them out?"

"Oh, yes please!" said Jenny enthusiastically.

Tina showed her how to put Daisy's head collar on and how to walk with her down the little lane which led to the mares' field. Jenny was a little nervous about actually going into the field; she had never been in such close proximity to so many horses at the same time before and she thought they all looked much bigger than they did in their stables. Tina showed her where to stand in relation to Daisy and how to unclip the lead rope and step back, which Jenny understood was in case the horse either jumped or kicked in excitement or, worse, barged into you the minute it was free. Daisy neither jumped nor barged, and Jenny felt a little pang of loss as she watched her blow down her nose, shake her head and, with her long thick white tail swishing from side to side in tune with the movement of her bottom, she strolled into the middle of the field, dropped her head and began to graze.

CHAPTER SIX

DAISY GOES TO
SUMMER CAMP

On the Saturday, Jenny once again joined Billie's group to go out for a hack, and this time they avoided the village and took the same route Tina had taken on the Thursday: a canter up The Cutting followed by a flat canter on the grass strip at the top of the hill. Daisy had yawned when Jenny arrived at her stable and, as it was a much warmer day, Jenny hoped it would be yet another mischief-free hack. This time, she did not fall off on the grass strip and instead was able to think more about how to pull Daisy up at the end of the canter. In actual fact, the riding school horses all seemed to understand that today they were in a group and all doing the same thing, so starting and stopping the canter was largely controlled by Billie and her mare, and Daisy slowed down at the end along with all the others. Jenny resolved to ask Tina if they could practise starting and stopping in the various paces so that she felt a bit more in control.

When Jenny got back to the yard, Billie took charge of turning the horses out and Jenny headed off to the office for a drink. Wendy, who answered the telephone and made a note of all the bookings for hacks and lessons, was on the telephone when she arrived.

"Hello," she said brightly when she had rung off, "how was your hack today?"

"I really enjoyed it," said Jenny. "I think hacking out on Daisy is really helping me."

"Good, good," said Wendy. "I might have a bit of bad news, then, but it's not too bad. Daisy has to go away for a week and when she comes back she will need a week off, so we shall have to find you a different horse for those two weeks. The good news is that there are plenty of sound horses like Daisy and, since the more horses you ride the more experience you have, it will probably help you in the long run."

"Where is she going?" asked Jenny in dismay. "Does she go away often?"

"No," replied Wendy, "this is the first time ever. She has been booked to go to Summer Camp by the mum of one of the little girls who has lessons on Saturdays, Felicity. It's a residential holiday for young riders, organised every summer by the local college. We have suggested that there are other ponies which are more suitable and which have been to Summer Camp, or events like it many times before and know the ropes, but Felicity adores Daisy and Mrs Nugent is adamant that she will take nothing else." Wendy shrugged her shoulders. "There is nothing I can do, I am afraid, but we can look at the list while you drink your coffee and you can have first choice of the other horses for the next two weeks."

Jenny collected her coffee from the machine and pulled up a chair as Wendy ran through the various names, some of which were familiar to Jenny as she had already ridden them in school. They decided that Annie would be a good choice, as she had, said Wendy, a nice smooth stride and was fairly quiet and had never been known to play up or misbehave either in school or out. Jenny felt relieved, as she had already ridden Annie once or twice and liked her. She was, if anything, easier to ride than Daisy, who had quite a bouncy trot. Jenny had had some difficulty getting used to a sitting trot on Daisy; and if she could not have Daisy for a few weeks, at least she had the comfort of knowing that the replacement was a horse she knew and liked. But two weeks?! It seemed an eternity! She had become extremely fond of Daisy and thought about her a lot when she was not at the yard. The week seemed to consist of looking forward to seeing her, enjoying the ride on her, thinking about how the ride had gone and then looking forward to the next one. She often thought of Daisy last thing at night before she went to sleep and first thing in the morning when she awoke.

Jenny's Thursday ride passed uneventfully. It was much cloudier and a little windy and, since Jenny had not ridden Annie on a hack before, Tina decided they would do something completely different and head out through the village towards the river and the woods. Seeing new territory pleased Jenny very much, as she had not realised that there was so much variety to be enjoyed. The river, the hills, the woods, there was a little copse at the end of the village, where there were a number of fallen trees for some jumping practice one day, when she had learned much more, and there were some lovely grass strips at the edges of fields as well. Tina told her that these were called lands and were used for canters when the weather was too bad for them to go up into the hills.

Jenny was booked into Billie's group hack as usual on the Saturday, but this time to ride Annie instead of Daisy. As she was making her usual tour of the yard and looking at the horses after arriving early, she heard a familiar sound behind her and turned to see Daisy's head hanging over her stable door.

"What are you doing here?" she asked. Not surprisingly there was no reply; Daisy merely returned to her little piles of hay.

Jenny immediately went off to the office to ask if she could ride Daisy instead of Annie. Wendy was busy with several new clients, taking their details and asking them to fill in forms for their insurance, and Jenny waited patiently. After about ten minutes the office was empty again.

"I thought I would see you this morning," said Wendy, grinning. "Yes, she's back, the little minx. Expelled from Summer Camp for unruly behaviour within forty-eight hours."

"What?" exclaimed Jenny. "What on earth did she do?"

"Well, it was more a case of what she didn't do," said Wendy wryly; "apparently no-one could do a thing with her. She was too much for Felicity, which didn't surprise us actually. It's one thing for a child who is learning to ride a horse in a group lesson when they all follow one another's tails, and quite another to be handling her independently of the group. I gather Daisy's worst offence was to jump the queue in the jumping lesson and go round the arena twice before anyone could stop her, by which time Felicity was on the floor and in tears."

"Oh dear…" Jenny trailed off, not knowing quite what to say. "Err… is it possible to ride her this morning instead of Annie?"

"Well, it might have been," said Wendy, "had Sally Pritchett not telephoned last night and spoken to the new girl who was in charge of the office for an hour while I went to bring some horses in. She took a booking for Sally and allocated Daisy to her. I'm afraid it would be unfair to ask her to change; she doesn't have the time to hack very often and, to be honest, she is a little heavy for Annie. Are you happy to proceed as planned? I can book you in for Daisy twice next week as usual…?"

Jenny could hardly refuse, so she agreed. She liked Sally Pritchett and had not seen her for a while. Sally was an air hostess and was rarely in the country for long enough to enjoy her passion for riding. She was extremely sociable and very good company, and Jenny thought that having a companion of her own age on the group hack almost made up for not riding Daisy.

CHAPTER SEVEN

SALLY AND ANNIE

S ally arrived at that moment and breezed into the office looking tanned and, thought Jenny, far more glamorous in her riding attire than Jenny could ever hope to look. Sally was much taller than Jenny and had long slim legs which looked fantastic in her navy jodhpurs. Her bright pink and navy top with sharp white collar and cuffs was one of the season's newest designs, and Jenny had admired it in the tack shop and wished she could afford it. Sally's thick blonde hair was expertly tied back into a tiny net, which kept it under control just beneath the back of her riding hat, and bright pink lipstick and matching nail polish completed the look.

"Hello, Jenny!" exclaimed Sally. "Good to see you! How are you? I hear you are making great progress."

"Well," said Jenny cautiously, "I am certainly making progress and I feel a little more confident but I don't want to tempt fate before a hack out."

Sally nodded her understanding. "Quite right too," she said with a grin. "Shall we see if the horses are ready for us?"

They went out to the yard to see some of the group already mounted, their horses standing patiently while Billie busied herself with getting everyone ready to leave.

In almost no time at all they were on their way and, after trotting energetically along the white chalk track most of the way to The Cutting, the horses were all blowing down their noses. Daisy and Annie had trotted happily side by side all the way up the track whilst Jenny told Sally all about Tina helping her to make progress with hacks out instead of lessons.

"Well, I expect you are much fitter to ride than me, then," said Sally; "my thigh muscles will be complaining about all this trotting tomorrow morning!"

Annie was much smoother than Daisy in every gait and Jenny found her very responsive. Billie had warned Jenny that Annie covered the ground quite quickly in canter because her stride was longer than Daisy's, so it might feel faster, but not to worry as she was such a good mare she would slow down immediately you put the slightest pressure on the rein. The group headed onto The Little Gallop for their second canter, and this time they lined up at the start side by side, leaving a reasonable width between each horse. Jenny and Annie were on the extreme left of the line, and Daisy and Sally were on their immediate right. Billie faced them all whilst checking that everyone was ready, then turned her own horse around to face up the strip and with a "Ready, everyone? One, two, three…" whilst simultaneously looking over her shoulder at them all, they set off.

They had only just transitioned to canter and made a few strides, when suddenly Daisy veered across Annie's path at a right angle. It took both Jenny and Annie completely by surprise and, as Annie pulled up to avoid colliding with Daisy and altered course to the left to get out of her way, Jenny saw the look of shock and surprise on Sally's face. At the same time, Daisy gave a skip to change legs and then leapt to the right and tore off up the strip at a gallop, leaving the rest of the group well behind. It took a second or two for Jenny to collect herself and gently turn Annie to follow the others, and by the time they reached the finish they were almost last.

"I am so sorry!" exclaimed Sally apologetically when Jenny reached her. "I promise you that was definitely not my doing; this naughty little mare ignored all my aids and I think she deliberately put you off so that she could get to the finish ahead of Annie. It's a long time since I have galloped that fast – gosh, I didn't think she would stop!"

"Whatever happened there?" asked Billie as she came over to them.

"Daisy deliberately altered course to put Jenny and Annie off. I think she was determined to beat Annie to the finish," replied Sally. "I'm really sorry, I really didn't intend to gallop, I just couldn't slow her down."

Billie shook her head. "Naughty girl, Daisy! Honestly, she is a real character. I have never known a riding school pony get up to so much mischief, and I have certainly never known one to scupper an opponent to beat them in a canter. Did you hear about the jumping lesson she hijacked the other day?"

Sally and Jenny shook their heads.

"Well, it was on Saturday. The weather was dreadful, and we had so many children booked into lessons, we split the big indoor school in half with a row of bales, two bales high, down the middle.

Sue had a group of the little ones riding in a circle and they had to make their ponies walk over a trotting pole at each side of the circle. Tina was giving a jumping lesson to a group of teenagers in the other side of the school. Daisy was in Sue's class with the little ones, and at one point in the lesson she obviously decided that Tina's lesson looked a lot more fun, so she jumped over the bales and went to join in. Fortunately, the little girl riding her stayed on and wasn't frightened by it, in fact she thought it was funny, so did the rest of the children."

Sally and Jenny laughed and, as they were chatting, the group left The Little Gallop and made their way back down the hill to the yard.

Chapter Eight

Problems in the Paddock

"Are you ladies in a rush today?" asked Billie once they had tied up the horses and were untacking. Sally and Jenny shook their heads.

"Well, I'm taking the jumping lesson for Tina today as she has to go to the dentist," said Billie. "Would you like to brush Annie and Daisy off and check their feet and turn them out for me? They have had a good hack and they are usually very good when you turn them out; they shouldn't be any problem."

Jenny nodded eagerly, and Sally said, "With pleasure. I had my own horse for a while a few years ago, so I know exactly what to do. We'll be fine."

Sally fetched the grooming equipment while Jenny took the saddles and bridles back to the tack room. She was fascinated by the tack room; it smelled of old leather and soap and polish and the faint odour of warm horses. The floor was dusty and the tiny window was in need of a clean – a bright shaft of sunlight beamed through it, highlighting the dust in the atmosphere. There were rows of racks for all the saddles, with a name under each one: Woody, Crumpet, Penny, Pansy; all the tiny saddles for the very small ponies were set on the bottom row where presumably little hands could reach to put them back. Daisy, Annie, Trooper, Penny, Roger... the names went on and on, as the medium-sized saddles spanned the next three rows for the majority of the larger ponies and small to medium sized horses which were used for lessons. The names on the top row were altogether more distinguished: General, Major, Ariadne, Winston, Horace, Charley; some of the larger horses were kept at livery and exercised by the staff, as their owners worked in the City and only came at weekends. Jenny finished stowing the tack, dropping the saddlecloths they had used into the washing basket, and went back to help Sally.

"Did you have your own horse for very long?" she asked.

Sally went on to explain that she'd had a half share with a friend when she was at university but that was a few years ago. She had actually spent more time caring for the horse than riding it as it was constantly off work owing to injuries. It had seemed very accident prone, especially in the paddock, and they eventually discovered that it had a problem with its eyesight and the vet advised them not to ride it again. Her friend had kept it and it lived out in the field with one of the older retired horses.

While Sally chatted, she was grooming Daisy, and showed Jenny how to safely stand to one side to comb Annie's tail and clean her feet. It was rare, she said, that a horse actually kicked out in either malice or surprise, but one kick could shatter your leg bone so it was best to follow good practice at all times. Once the mares were ready, the girls strolled down to the gate at the end of the lane in the warm sunlight. The large rectangular paddock where Annie and Daisy were kept contained about twenty-five mares, and most of them were scattered around the ground, heads down, grazing quietly. One or two had their backs to the fence and were facing the sun, eyes closed, tails swishing to deter any flies.

There was a water trough quite close to the entry gate and a ring of horses around it, standing quietly but not close enough to be able to drink. Sally unlatched the gate and took Daisy in first, leaving Jenny and Annie just outside. She released Daisy, who blew down her nose, and, after taking one or two steps towards the trough, stood still with one fetlock bent in a relaxed pose. Sally came back through the gate and took Annie from Jenny and, once released in the paddock, Annie strolled around the other side of the trough and wandered out to the middle of the field before dropping her head to graze.

"I wonder what they are all waiting for?" mused Sally.

They soon found out. There was a smaller horse, a bay of about 12 hands, with a white star on its forehead, which had apparently fallen asleep with its head lolling over the trough. Next to it was a thin chestnut with four white socks, about the same size. The girls watched as one of the other horses quietly approached the trough and attempted to drink from it, and the thin chestnut promptly rushed over to it, with its ears pinned right back and neck stretched out, to chase it away. It looked as if the chestnut was guarding the little bay which had gone to sleep. One of the other mares, a grey, then stepped forward and tried to get to the trough for a drink, but had hardly taken two paces when the same thing happened. With a squeal and a gnashing of teeth, the chestnut flew at it with head outstretched and ears flat and forced it to step back.

"What a nuisance," said Sally. "It's so hot, they all need to drink. I wonder how long this has been going on this afternoon."

"Should we tell one of the yard staff?" asked Jenny.

"Let's just stand and watch for a minute or two to see if things change," said Sally. "If not, then yes, I think we should."

As she was speaking, Daisy took one step forward and blew down her nose, then stopped and rested the other hind leg. A second or two later, she repeated the action. It seemed to Jenny that Daisy was trying to sneak up to the trough bit by bit whilst demonstrating at the same time that she was in no rush and feeling very relaxed about it. The chestnut did not seem to notice her, at least it did not react. When Daisy was almost at the trough, she stretched out her neck to drink, but the chestnut hurtled around from the other side of the trough in a flash and charged at her. Daisy quickly turned 180 degrees, perhaps to defend herself with her hind legs if necessary, but then moved slowly back towards the outer circle again instead. However, instead of standing still, she walked around the outside of the circle until she was positioned exactly opposite where she had been standing the first time and, again, stopped and rested one hind leg. She repeated her previous attempt, step by step, resting between movements, until she was right next to the trough; but as she began to drop her head to drink, the chestnut once again squealed and charged at her, this time forcing her to back away. She stopped where she was and stood quite still for a few moments, her tail swishing from side to side, surveying the scene and watching the chestnut whilst it took up its original position again, guarding the bay mare.

Daisy continued to look in the direction of the trough and the thirsty group around it for another minute or two before turning away and finally heading out towards the middle of the paddock. Sally and Jenny were about to move away from the gate and go back to the yard to tell them what was happening, when they heard another squeal and the girls turned just in time to see Daisy spin 180 degrees in one swift movement and canter quickly towards the trough, directly towards the bay which had fallen asleep! Some of the horses standing in the circle around the trough, disturbed by the sudden energetic movement, shuffled their feet and fidgeted, and the little bay awoke with a start, saw Daisy heading straight for her and turned and galloped away up the other side of the paddock, hotly pursued by her chestnut guardian. All the horses waiting around the trough then moved in, and one by one quenched their thirst with a lovely long drink.

"Clever lass!" exclaimed Sally, grinning. "What a great example of lateral thinking! You can imagine them all saying, 'Thanks, Daisy'."

Jenny was impressed and felt very proud of her four-legged friend. She felt a pang of remorse that she had missed a hack on her today but consoled herself with the thought that, had Daisy had the two weeks off as previously arranged, Jenny could not have ridden her for another ten days, whereas their hack was in the diary for Thursday – and she was looking forward to it already!

CHAPTER NINE

LONGER HACKS

Over the next few weeks, Jenny's confidence grew. Tina spent some time helping Jenny refine her position and balance during their hacks, and now she could control the speed of all three paces – walk, trot and canter – and could make the transitions from one pace to another fairly smoothly as well. She needed to practise her transition from canter back to trot as she still found Daisy very bouncy, but the plus side was that Daisy's trot was very rhythmic and the speed was just right. Consequently, when they trotted for some distance, Jenny found the trot easy to maintain and she was developing strength in her leg muscles.

One Wednesday evening when Jenny was at home, Tina telephoned to ask if she would like to hack out for longer on the Thursday morning, perhaps for two hours instead of one.

"Gosh, yes!" replied Jenny excitedly. "Any particular reason?"

"Well, Wendy is arranging a fundraising charity ride for a few weeks' time," said Tina. "I wondered if you might like to join in? It is quite expensive, but lots of clients will want to go, and if you would like to come we need to book Daisy for you straight away in case someone else beats you to it. In addition, you need to have some experience of being in the saddle for more than an hour, and I thought we could try two hours for starters tomorrow and see how you get on. What do you think? I can give you more information tomorrow."

"Two hours sounds like heaven," replied Jenny. "Is that how long the charity ride will be for?"

"Errr, no," Tina giggled, "it is actually seven hours…"

"Seven hours?" said Jenny with surprise. "Good grief – what if I need to go to the toilet? What about—?"

"Panic not," Tina interrupted her. "We will stop about every two hours for everyone to have a leg stretch and some refreshment. It is a long day and, yes, you will be very tired afterwards, but if you can do it, the experience will be wonderful. I promise I will give you all the details tomorrow. Shall we meet at 10 a.m. instead of 11 a.m.?"

Jenny readily agreed and rang off. Seven hours! Gosh, that would be incredible. She could think of nothing else all evening, she had so many questions she wanted to ask. Where would they be going for seven hours? Would she need to take some lunch? What should she wear? What if it rained? Was she herself capable enough to join a long group ride? What if she panicked or fell off? What if she fell off and was injured? What if Daisy went lame? Was Daisy able to undertake such a long ride? Jenny's mind was still in a whirl when she went to bed, and she drifted off to sleep still thinking about it all. She dreamed she was cantering over endless hilltops, on and on and on, the sun on her face and Daisy beneath her, covering the ground as smoothly as if she were flying.

By 9 a.m. the next morning, Jenny was already outside Daisy's stable and, having been greeted by the now familiar nickering sound, was standing at the door scratching Daisy behind her ears, which Daisy seemed to like very much. Tina walked past her pushing a wheelbarrow piled high with clean straw.

"Hi," she said. "I am almost finished with mucking out. If you can please grab me a coffee, I'll be indoors in five minutes and we can have a natter before we tack up."

Jenny did as asked and was sitting in the sun on the bench outside the office sipping her hot sweet coffee when Tina arrived.

"Perfect, thanks," said Tina, producing a packet of chocolate biscuits. "Now, about this charity ride."

Jenny listened carefully while Tina explained the format for the charity ride day. The lorries would leave the yard at 8 a.m. sharp. There were saddle racks and hooks for bridles in a large compartment in each lorry so that the horses could travel in just travelling rugs and with head collars. The journey to the departure point would take about thirty minutes, then everyone would tack up their own horse. There would be toilet facilities at that stop. The ride would commence at 9 a.m., with a short refreshment stop at 11 a.m. (no toilets but plenty of bushes); lunch at 1 p.m. at a picnic site, which had proper rails for the horses to be tethered to, and then later on a tea break at around 3 p.m. They would cover a variety of terrain: very roughly, the first leg was farmland, the second included some ancient woodland, the third was open moorland and the fourth climbed first uphill and then wound down some narrow tracks to the sea.

"The sea?!" exclaimed Jenny. "I once saw a group of riders canter along a beach. It looked such fun. I have always longed to do that."

"Well, if anyone has any energy left at the end of twenty-five miles you might be able to!" replied Tina. "But first things first. Let's see how you get on with a two-hour hack."

Jenny found the longer ride surprisingly easy and the time passed quickly. They walked the horses more than usual and were able to have three canters instead of their usual two, after doubling back down the hill and over to the other side of the village for the third, where Tina had previously shown Jenny the grassy strips along the sides of some of the fields. Daisy was in good form, and when they had their third canter, instead of deferring to Missy and following behind in the usual way, Daisy skipped out and cantered alongside, keeping pace but staying slightly in front by about a head.

"Sorry," said Jenny, "she was a bit quick for me there. These little skips she does before she gets into mischief always catch me out; I never see or feel them coming."

"It's all right," replied Tina, "but just shorten your rein a little and don't let her get any further ahead of Missy, otherwise we'll have a race on our hands. Miss Daisy has been a bit full of herself this week and I am not entirely sure I trust her. Once we get to that big oak tree on our right we can both start to slow down at the same time, OK?"

Jenny nodded, concentrating and feeling just a bit vulnerable. She was beginning to flag just a little and did not want to end her first long hack either on a bad note or with a big challenge!

She need not have worried; the mares obediently slowed simultaneously at the big oak tree and blew down their noses contentedly as the girls walked them back through the village on long reins, home to the yard for their tea.

Over the next few weeks, two-hour rides became a regular Thursday feature and, to Jenny's delight, it gave them enough time to visit new territory. There was the wild flower nature reserve, with its rich colours, the hum of bees collecting nectar and a ford with an iron bridge adjacent to it, where they waded the horses through the water, laughing at the amount of splashing eight big hooves could produce. They rode along the main road for the first time, taking a shortcut through the sawmill yard with its tall piles of long tree trunks, rich smell of freshly cut wood and big scary yellow machines.

Jenny became totally immersed in developing her riding style and thought of little else. She bought a book in the tack shop which gave her hints on how to ride, and she discussed it with Tina. It all sounded remarkably easy in theory, and Tina pointed out that, generally, these instructions were of great use in school. However, wind, cattle, high spirits, soft ground, sudden noises – none of these things were mentioned as challenges to be overcome and only time in the saddle and practice could teach you how to deal with them. They also spent some time dealing with the horses in their stables. Tina helped Jenny practise tacking-up and un-tacking, tying up and untying, putting travel rugs on and taking them off, until she could do all these tasks quickly and efficiently.

CHAPTER TEN

THE DAY OF THE CHARITY RIDE

On the day of the charity ride, Jenny awoke at 6 a.m., just before her alarm went off. She leapt out of bed and pulled back the curtain only to see, to her dismay, a dreary grey drizzle and leaden skies. Throughout the summer she had been really lucky with the weather for her hacks. They had had the odd cloudy day, and once they'd had to cut short the hack and spent the last thirty minutes in an empty outdoor arena at the yard instead, as it looked very much as if it would pour with rain at any minute. She had never ridden on such a gloomy and damp day as this though, and her heart sank.

A quick look at the weather app on her phone whilst she ate her breakfast cheered her a little, as it appeared that the wet spell was passing through from west to east and, as they were heading west, with a bit of luck they might escape the worst of the weather. She had time for a lovely long, hotter-than-usual shower, which Tina had told her was good for warming muscles before a long time in the saddle, then dressed quickly and drove over to the yard. Tina had recommended she wear layers of clothing, as she could always take things off and either tie them around her waist or leave them in the van at the next refreshment stop. A new lightweight waterproof which packed into a tiny bag neatly hung around her waist, and she had a little pouch in her pocket containing tissues, lip gloss, a comb, a couple of plasters and some cream in case she was bitten or stung.

The yard was buzzing with activity, and Jenny felt a shiver of excitement and, at the same time, the familiar tummy-churning nervousness she had had when first learning to ride. She went straight to Daisy's stable and found Tina already there.

"Good morning!" Tina said cheerily. "Madam is nearly ready for you. She had a bath yesterday – doesn't she look glam?" Tina ran her fingers through Daisy's shining silky mane. "She's just finishing her breakfast." Daisy lifted her head briefly from her feed bowl and tossed it in Jenny's direction whilst making a sound like 'urggg'. The girls laughed.

"It's rude to speak with your mouth full, Daisy," said Tina, patting her affectionately on the wither. "I need a coffee, Jenny, I haven't had time for one yet. Why don't you come over to the office with me whilst Daisy finishes her food, and I can fill you in on some of the details of the day."

Jenny declined a coffee, fearing that toilet stops were a bit infrequent for her liking and not wanting the embarrassment of having to ask if the ride could stop for her convenience, which is what Tina had told her she would have to do in an emergency. She listened intently while Tina briskly ran through some last-minute instructions. There were twenty-two riders in all – sixteen clients and six staff – two ten-horse lorries, a two-horse trailer and the minibus which had two non-riding staff as back-up in case of an accident. Possessions could therefore be left safely in the minibus, which would be attended at all times, and it also contained first-aid kits for both horses and riders and, most importantly, food and drink.

"I also want to give you some last-minute tips on riding in a big group like this," said Tina, sipping her coffee. "All the riding school horses have been on rides like this before. They are generally happy to be part of the group. After the first stop they will have worn off their initial freshness. It is unusual for any horse to bolt and leave the group and, as well as we six staff, there are some very good riders with us today, so I think a 'cavalry charge' most unlikely. However, we will be having a canter or two, and I have put a neck strap in with Daisy's tack so that in an emergency you can hold on tight; I know you prefer that to the idea of grabbing a chunk of mane. If you have any problem, or feel remotely unsafe, tuck Daisy in behind the biggest horse's bottom nearest to you, hold onto your neck strap, check your position and balance, keep your heels down, take a deep breath and relax. Clear?"

Jenny nodded her agreement. She was feeling more nervous with every passing moment and was glad when they left the office so that she could visit the toilet one last time. The big horseboxes were parked near the yard gate, and already the staff were loading the horses onto them. Jenny looked on as each horse clattered up the metal ramps, and she thought how smart they all looked, immaculately groomed with shining manes and tails, brightly coloured travel rugs and tail wraps, coloured pads around their legs and matching head collars. Daisy, Jenny thought, looked especially pretty in a bright red rug which made a beautiful contrast with her black and white piebald markings.

The convoy left the yard promptly at 8 a.m. and wound its way very slowly through the village and out into the open countryside where the land was quite flat in comparison to their local hills. After about half an hour they pulled into a large car park next to a wooden building, and Jenny recognised it as a tourist spot, where there were both routes for walking and cycling around a big lake, and a large adventure playground for children. As the horses were unloaded from the lorries they were tied to rails which had been installed especially for visiting riders, and the riding school staff handed out saddles and bridles to the clients. Jenny was pleased that she had had so much practice with tacking-up and untacking, as she was shaking with nerves and her fingers and thumbs fumbled clumsily with all the buckles and straps. Daisy looked around with interest and chomped absentmindedly on the cold metal bit in her mouth. The sky had cleared a little and the occasional glimpse of blue was visible between the thick, fluffy white clouds.

Wendy was leading the ride on General, a rather grand 18-hand Irish Draught with impeccable manners and a sweet nature. She had raised him from a foal and he was her pride and joy. They had competed in many county competitions, and a row of silver cups and medals decorated the wall behind Wendy's desk in the office. Jenny already knew Billie, Sue and Tina but not Polly, who managed the horses and dealt with their general care, feeding and stabling back at the yard. The sixth member of staff was a new girl called Karen, about seventeen years old. Jenny had said hello to her once or twice and found her rather shy.

There were four riders who had brought their own horses, classy event horses which rippled with muscle and looked very fit, and four children on smaller ponies. Jenny recognised the children as being the four good little riders who joined Billie's Saturday hack every week. Ed, another Saturday rider, was on Olly as usual; there were three girls who arrived together every Friday for a group lesson, Julie, Lindsey and Helen. Then there were the local farmer's sons, Tom and Nathan, good riders whom Jenny assumed had begun to ride as soon as they could walk. The last rider was a woman Jenny had not seen before, Alice, who was riding Annie, so Jenny supposed she might be a beginner like herself. The minibus was driven by Alan, a big red-faced man who usually drove the tractor and delivered the hay and straw for the horses, and his wife Joy was in charge of the refreshments.

Jenny was still feeling shaky as she mounted, but once they were on their way she began to relax and enjoy the sights and smells around her. It was late August and the fields were full of crops which would soon be harvested. The trees were beginning to look tired, their once bright green leaves starting to dull as they lost their moisture under the summer sun, and stray stems of barley, blown by the wind when the field was sown, brushed against the horses' legs as they rode along the green field edges. At one point, Daisy stopped abruptly to reach for a blackberry in the hedge, and Annie, who was directly behind them, almost bumped into her.

"Steady, Daisy!" said Alice, who had lurched forward over Annie's neck at the sudden stop. "Haven't you had any breakfast?"

"Do you know her, then?" asked Jenny.

"Yes," said Alice, "I had her once in school and she gave me a terrible time. I never wanted to ride her again after that; she was too lively for me."

"What on earth did she do?" enquired Jenny.

"Well, she had apparently misbehaved in a previous group lesson and, as a result, Sue had told the little girl who was riding her that if Daisy broke rank and cantered off with her again, she should ride her straight into a corner as then she couldn't possibly do anything else but stop."

"Goodness," said Jenny, "what a naughty little mare."

"Well, yes," replied Alice, "but unfortunately Daisy thought that being driven into the corner was a highly amusing new game, and every time we tried to transition from trot to canter, she remembered it and tore off towards the furthest corner of the indoor school and slammed on the brakes. I nearly shot over her head twice."

Jenny giggled. "Sorry to laugh," she said. "I do sympathise and, yes, she can be a little mischievous."

Alice came alongside so that they could chat more easily, and Jenny told her about Daisy having a pee while they were hacking; being sent home from Summer Camp in disgrace; how she had jumped over the bales in the indoor school to join the jumping lesson; and how she had tried to be first at the end of the canter on the hill by deliberately making Annie veer off course.

Jenny was amazed at how quickly the first two hours passed and was very glad of the coffee and pastries offered at the first refreshment stop, as breakfast seemed a very long time ago. There was nowhere to tie the horses so the riders took it in turns to hold one another's mounts while the other finished a pastry. There were, as Tina had promised, plenty of bushes, and Alan and Joy, who had been following the ride by road before waiting for them in a clearing, held onto the horses while people made themselves more comfortable.

When they set off again, Wendy began moving up and down the line of horses as the ride progressed, making sure that both horses and riders were comfortable and chatting briefly to everyone before moving on again. Billie was at the back of the ride with the four event horses and their owners: Sue was with Julie, Lindsey and Helen; Polly was with the four smaller ponies; and Tina was with the three boys. Jenny and Alice found themselves second and third in line behind Karen, who was riding Spice. Jenny remembered Spice arriving at the yard – a large jet black four-year-old gelding with flowing mane and tail and enormous hooves. He had shown great promise as a showjumper but was very green under saddle, and he was often being pushed around by the other geldings in the paddock. He had blossomed during his time at the yard but was still quite nervous and inexperienced. Once he had joined the Saturday hack and Billie had had to give the client her own horse and ride Spice instead, as he kept shying at the slightest thing.

CHAPTER ELEVEN

SPICE AND THE IRON BATH

Karen clearly liked Spice and rode him a lot. Jenny wondered whether they were two of a kind, as Karen was also young and a little inexperienced – perhaps they were kindred spirits? As they approached a little copse they naturally fell into single file again, as the path was very narrow in places. Daisy was directly behind Spice, and they had not gone very far when Spice reared very slightly, lowered his bottom and backed towards Daisy, causing Jenny to pull her over to the left onto rough

grass to avoid him. Karen spoke to him quietly and urged him to ride forward again, but he had only taken a step or two before the same thing happened again, and this time he was trying to bend his body around as if to run back to where he had come from. From her position on the left, Jenny could see what the problem was – there was a big iron bath which had been dumped in the undergrowth and it was partly overgrown with brambles. It had large carved feet which looked rather like lion's paws. Spice must have thought it was some terrible monster waiting to pounce. Karen tried to urge him past it, speaking more firmly this time, but it seemed to make matters worse and he lifted his front feet off the ground as if he really was going to rear.

"What's going on?" called Wendy from way behind them.

Jenny turned to see where Wendy was and, as she did so, she felt Daisy move beneath her. Daisy walked forwards until her head was level with Spice's shoulder and reached over to nuzzle him gently on the neck; she then took a step forward to place herself between Spice and the iron bath and nuzzled him again. He turned to look at her, then slowly and carefully made a step forwards; at the same time, Daisy stepped forward to match his progress. Little by little they passed the obstacle but, with Spice still clearly leading the ride, and once they were clear, Daisy slowed again and dropped back into position behind him. Jenny leaned forward and gave Daisy a big pat on her neck.

"You really are a star!" she whispered, and she felt a pricking sensation behind her eyes as she did so.

The woodland became thicker and soon they were riding on quite a wide path, with a dark canopy of branches above them and thick bracken on either side. It seemed very quiet; *too quiet*, thought Jenny. It was almost eerie, and she shivered at the sudden drop in temperature. From time to time they passed a clearing where trees had been felled and laid in piles, and then the clearings began to appear more frequently, until they reached a picnic site. There were barbecues and lots of wooden benches around, the kind with bench seats attached. Alan and Joy were already there waiting for them; and as everyone dismounted, Alan and Joy took two horses each, popped head collars on them, walked them to the rails, tied them up and loosened their girths. All the riders were glad to stretch their legs and walk around horse-free for a few minutes after four hours in the saddle. There were several families at the picnic site and the horses did not seem to mind the children shouting and playing. Jenny was starving and tucked into her lunch with relish, eating far more sandwiches than she usually did, and washing them down with fizzy water from a cool box.

"How is it going?" asked Tina beside her. "Are you enjoying it?"

"It's absolutely fantastic!" replied Jenny and told her about Spice and the iron bath.

Tina nodded. "Daisy certainly does seem to have a kind heart. It's interesting that she made sure Spice was leading the whole time rather than taking the lead herself, as she did with Cara. I wonder if she has ever had a foal of her own. You know, I suspect she has."

They stopped for a full hour, which gave everyone time to have as much to eat and drink as they wanted and also to move around and chat to other riders. Jenny found herself talking to Lindsey, Helen and Julie and found that they had all started riding lessons together, about two years previously, and they all worked together at a bank in the local town. All three were very jolly and sociable, and Jenny thought it would be good fun to have them on a Saturday hack one day. She had really enjoyed the day that Sally had joined her.

Chapter Twelve

Naughty Ponies

Once lunch was over, they continued riding in the forest until it gave way to open moorland with sparse heathers, coarse grass and quite a few very large stones, almost boulders, dotted around. Wendy, who was at the front of the ride again, called back to them.

"Is everyone OK for a canter?" The group collectively murmured an assurance that they were. "Right, let's trot to the other side of that clump of bushes," she said, pointing, "and then we'll canter as far as the three trees. I set the pace, no-one is to pass me please and no racing one another – agreed?"

Again the response was a murmur of agreement.

Wendy set off at a trot with the group spread out behind her, and Jenny was pleased to be having a change of pace. She had never cantered in such a large group before and it felt quite exciting and free in comparison to the more controlled canters she had experienced on group hacks. She was concentrating on her position and feeling pleased that Daisy was not too lively, when she noticed that to their left was a small herd of wild ponies which had seen the group cantering and was heading directly for them.

At the same time as the herd reached their left flank, one of the four little girls on a pony started to race past the other three, giggling. As she overtook one of the others, her own pony kicked out at it and its rider screamed. The herd, spooked by the sudden noise, turned and galloped off to the left; the pony which had kicked out raced after them as if to catch them up, and the other three ponies turned and followed as well. Jenny watched in horror and was wondering what on earth would happen next, when Daisy began to gain speed, jumped a boulder which was in her way and veered left to follow the herd.

"No, Daisy, NO!" shouted Jenny, trying to pull her up, but Daisy was much too strong for her and she could do nothing but maintain her position, concentrate on her balance and hold tight onto the neck strap, as Tina had previously advised. She felt quite helpless, and tears began to well up behind her eyes as she suddenly felt very frightened at being out of control. Daisy continued to head to the left of the herd and, with a skip to change her diagonal, began to veer to the right, moving very close to the ponies on her own immediate right. She tossed her head at them, ears flat back, and the ponies also moved over towards the right, in turn forcing the ones next to them to do the same. Within a second or two, the entire little herd began to turn to the right, with the four little girls in the middle of the herd galloping flat out and giggling, clearly enjoying themselves, oblivious to any apparent danger.

Wendy and the rest of the group had reached the trees and stopped and were standing in a line facing the approaching herd. As the herd approached the trees, Daisy sped up to get ahead of it and, once in front, threw her back legs out in a kind of buck as if to kick the ponies immediately behind her, then she tossed her head again to the right, with ears flat back. As she did so, she began to slow down. The ponies directly behind her drew back to avoid Daisy's buck and began to reduce speed, and as she gradually slowed down, so did they. Their trot slowed to a walk as they approached Wendy's line and, rather than get too near, they scattered and wandered off individually to graze. Tina and Polly came from either side of Wendy's line to supervise the four little girls and get them back into the group. Daisy blew down her nose and shook her head, her sides heaving.

"Are you OK?" Tina asked Jenny anxiously.

"Yes, I think so," replied Jenny, feeling the tears fall in spite of her efforts to contain them. She immediately felt silly and self-conscious and wiped her eyes with the back of a gloved hand. It had been quite a shock being suddenly 'taken off with' like that for the first time.

"No harm done," said Tina sympathetically, "and you coped very well – I was very impressed that you stayed on when she jumped the boulder!"

"Well, I didn't actually do anything," said Jenny. "I just kept my position, and it happened so quickly I didn't have time to think about it."

"Give her a good pat and a rub," said Tina quietly, nodding at Daisy, "she's earned it. In spite of her occasional mischief, our Daisy has a very good brain and a lot of common sense, and for what it's worth she doesn't have an ounce of malice in her. Most horses understand that their job is partly to keep their rider safe and she knew exactly what she was doing. I don't believe she would have taken off like that if she didn't think you could ride it safely. And she was right, wasn't she?"

"I suppose so," replied Jenny with a watery smile. She knew Tina was trying to make her feel better and didn't want to dwell on how wobbly and upset she actually felt.

The ride moved off again and they made their way across the heathland, passing the occasional wild pony or donkey, but fortunately no more small herds. The ponies seemed to have burned off a bit of excess energy with their gallop and were much less fidgety, and their young riders settled down as well. Daisy also seemed very relaxed and Jenny let her have a long rein so that she could stretch her neck right down to the ground. The clouds had rolled away and the air seemed much warmer. Every so often they came across a pretty picture-postcard cottage in an idyllic spot, with its facade bathed in sunlight and pink roses growing around the door. They turned off the little lane towards a small hamlet with a row of cottages and an old village inn with a thatched roof. There was a large car park next to the inn and a long sturdy rail, perfect for tying up the horses.

Alan and Joy were already there to greet them and had erected a small picnic table which was laden with bottles of drinks, fresh fruit and deliciously thick pieces of cake. After about fifteen minutes they set off again and began to climb uphill and, as they passed through a large open gateway, a soft green grass slope stretched upwards and away from them.

"Is everyone OK for another canter?" asked Wendy. "Less exciting than the last one, if you please!"

The group murmured their agreement and Jenny noticed that Sue and Polly moved over to flank the four ponies this time, just in case! There was ample space, and the rest of the group fanned out in a long line. The canter was really enjoyable and Jenny felt her confidence and equilibrium return. Since they were heading uphill, it was just a little harder for the horses, especially as they had already covered three quarters of the ride; but because of that, the speed was just right, thought Jenny. She found it very easy indeed to pull up.

At the top of the hill they could see the glint of the sea in the distance and there was a long low stone wall in front of them with a gate wide enough for one horse to pass through at a time. The breeze was stronger up here and they passed through a field full of grazing sheep which seemed unconcerned by their presence. They began their descent by joining a narrow sandy path which wove in and out of spiky gorse-like bushes. As the hill became steeper, they naturally slowed down because the horses were having to pick their way very carefully. Every now and then a loose stone clattered past them and bounced away towards the bottom.

At the base of the hill was a large iron gate and, once they had passed through it, there was a grassy verge which bordered the hill, and a tarmac lane alongside. They trotted for a few hundred yards along the lane before reaching another little hamlet, this time with a row of cottages which looked like fishermen's cottages. To their right they could see that the sea was much closer now, and as they made their way through the tiny village street the tangy smell of saltwater and seaweed hung in the air. Eventually, they came to an old cobbled slipway worn smooth over time, with large iron rings set into the stones and a small collection of old boats of varying sizes. Some of them were covered with tarpaulins, others contained the sort of pots used for catching lobster and shellfish.

Wendy called for the group to halt and said, "OK, everyone, we have arrived at the beach! We will have a short canter along the shoreline between the flags, but only in single file – can everyone see the flags…? Good. Once we get to the line of buoys which you can see roped together over there," she waved her hand to the right, "you can go into the sea if you would like to wash your horse's legs and let them cool off. Please can you all stay reasonably close together? There are people walking dogs along here and some children making sandcastles; we don't want to frighten anyone. Any questions?"

There were none, and the riders eagerly followed Wendy down to the shoreline near to the first flag where the canter began. Jenny found the canter exhilarating; it was long and straight and there was a much stiffer breeze on the shoreline. Drops of spray flew up all around her as the hooves of the horse in front splashed through the foam at the water's edge.

Wendy slowed the ride in good time before the line of buoys and some of the horses bent their heads to dip their noses into the water, snorting when they realised it was not the sort of taste they were used to. The ponies were the first to go in up to their tummies, again supervised by Sue and Polly in case they went in too deep. Daisy seemed to know what to do and Jenny thought she must have seen the sea before. She waded in until the sea was up to her tummy, her thick long white tail swirling behind her in the water. She too dropped her head and blew down her nose into the sea, shaking her head. After a few minutes the first horses started to make their way back onto the beach, where everyone loosened their reins so they could all stretch and relax.

Daisy fidgeted from one foot to another before dropping to her knees, which took Jenny by surprise.

"Get off! Get off!" yelled Wendy and Sue together. "She's going to roll!"

Everyone laughed as Tina quickly jumped off Missy, handed Karen her rein and hurried towards Daisy to grab her reins and stop her from rolling, while Jenny dismounted and stood beside them both.

Tina held Daisy tightly and said, "That was lucky. If they roll with a saddle on, that's bad enough as it can break the saddle tree, but I would hate to see one roll with a rider on board!"

After a while they left the beach and retraced their steps past the fishermen's cottages and up to a crossroads. They turned right, and after a few minutes Jenny could see the trailer and minibus in a nearby field. The horse transport had been moved to the finishing point by Wendy and Polly's husbands and Polly's son. They had been driven by car to the starting point and were now travelling home as extra passengers in the minibus, while three staff travelled in each horsebox. Alan and Joy greeted them all warmly and congratulated them on their achievement. For the next thirty minutes, everyone was very busy untacking their horses and making them comfortable, washing their tummies and legs with fresh water brought from the horseboxes in large containers. Jenny gave Daisy a good brush, washed her legs, checked her feet and combed her mane but was unable to do a great deal more with her salty tail than swish it around in a big circle to get rid of most of the moisture.

"It's a warm day," said Tina next to her, attending to Missy, "it will soon dry, and we can do a better job once we get home. They just need to be comfortable enough to travel."

Before long all the horses were dressed for the journey again, with their coloured rugs, padded leg protection and tail bandages, and were led onto the lorry one by one where nets full of haylage were already tied up in front of them. Alan and Joy went around the riders offering them cups of tea or coffee from large flasks and handing out bars of chocolate. Jenny suddenly realised how tired she was and was grateful when they all took up their places in the various vehicles ready for the journey home. She closed her eyes briefly and could easily have fallen asleep had Alice not taken the seat beside her and begun to chatter excitedly about what a good day it had been.

As it was almost 7:30 p.m. by the time they got home and there were only a few staff left at the yard, Wendy asked if all the adult riders would mind taking their horses to their respective stables. Daisy and Missy were two of the last to be unloaded, and Jenny and Tina walked the mares together to their stables in the middle of the old cobbled yard. Jenny put Daisy in her stable and the mare stood patiently while the head collar, tail wrap and travelling boots were removed. For once, she did not seem too interested in the contents of her feed bowl. Jenny stood stroking Daisy's neck and running her fingers through the thick silky mane.

"Thank you, Daisy," she said. "I had a lovely day and you were a very, very good girl for me."

Daisy turned her head to look at Jenny and dropped her soft pink velvet nose into Jenny's hands for her to stroke her some more. It was several minutes before Jenny felt they were being watched and looked over her shoulder to see Tina with her elbows on the door, chin resting on her hands.

"You two make a good team, you know," she said. "It's a very special thing to have that kind of connection with a riding school pony, they see so many riders, but I've always thought that she really likes you. Do you remember that day you fell off and she stopped instantly and waited for you?"

Jenny smiled. "I just love her to bits. I think about her all the time."

Daisy's head was beginning to drop and her lower lip wobbled a little.

Tina said briskly, "Come on, then, it's time I locked up; these ladies need their sleep and so do I." She yawned. "Two-hour hack on Thursday?" she asked as Jenny gave Daisy a final pat and left her stable. "Yes please," replied Jenny, thinking what a long way off Thursday sounded.

Jenny had never seen the yard at night before – there were security lights dotted about and a generally peaceful air about the place. The dark shadows of the horses grazing in the paddocks could just be made out in the dusky light, and from the stables nearest to Jenny's car came the rhythmic sound of horses chewing their hay. The air smelled sweet and the breeze had dropped. *How peaceful*, thought Jenny, as she drove out of the yard and headed for home, feeling very satisfied indeed with her day.

CHAPTER THIRTEEN

DAISY ON LOAN

The next time Jenny went up to the yard, she arrived early as usual. Tina happened to be outside the office sipping her coffee when Jenny pulled up in her car.

"Hi Jenny! Do you fancy a coffee?" called Tina as she approached. "I was just having a break." After saying hello to Wendy in the office and choosing hot chocolate, her favourite, from the drinks machine, Jenny joined Tina on the bench outside.

"Are you having a good week?" asked Tina.

"Yes, it's fine, thank you," replied Jenny, wondering why she was asking.

"I have a suggestion to make to you and something for you to think about as well," said Tina thoughtfully. "It's obvious that you really enjoy riding Daisy and she seems to really like you too. You have made a great deal of progress since you've been riding her, and I wonder if you might consider having her on loan?"

"Having her on loan?" replied Jenny. "I don't exactly know what you mean."

"Well, do you remember Carole, who used to join your lessons with Sue when you first started? She rode a horse called Barney."

"I remember," said Jenny. "Barney was her own horse. He was really sweet."

"Well, she didn't actually own him, he was on loan to her from the riding school," said Tina. "Like you, she was riding for a few hours a week, and it was cheaper for her to have Barney on loan, and pay for his food and lodgings, than it was to pay for several hacks and a lesson each week. Lots of people who ride only come now and then, perhaps in the spring and summer, or maybe join in with a weekly lesson in school. The loan arrangement is for people who want to ride more often, and it also benefits us, as the customer pays for shoes and does the mucking out at the weekends. We continue to use Barney for clients, as Carole sometimes works weekends, so he makes money for the school in that way as well. If you want staff to accompany you on hacks or give you lessons, you pay a discounted rate. You sign a contract with the school and it can be ended with a month's notice from either the school or the client at any time."

Jenny's head was spinning. "Gosh, I don't know – I had no idea such a thing existed, I thought you either had to have your own horse or visit a riding school. Would I still be able to ride with you on Thursdays?"

"Yes, of course," grinned Tina, "but it would be cheaper, and you could also join in any other group hacks, such as Billie's for example, for a reduced rate as well. Oh yes, and if any of the staff are exercising horses, you can join them for free. I often exercise some of the bigger horses myself. And of course you can ride with any of the staff in their free time, or other clients, such as Carole, who either have their own horses or horses on loan."

"I would need to see some figures on paper," said Jenny, "and if I could afford it, then yes – wow – I really would be interested. What do you think Daisy would say?"

"Well, you can ask her if you like," said Tina, standing up. "Karen is tacking her up for us so that I had time for a chat with you. Shall we go?"

They went through to the cobbled yard where Daisy was standing with her head hanging over the door, chewing her hay which had become entangled in her bit and was hanging out of the side of her mouth.

"Daisy, you can't take that with you, you know," said Tina, tugging at the soggy remainder of Daisy's mouthful as she led her out of the stable.

Jenny's head was in a whirl and her tummy felt as if it were full of butterflies. She felt a mixture of shock, surprise, excitement and elation all at the same time, tinged with anxiety that she might not be able to afford a loan arrangement long-term. She had so many questions she wanted to ask Tina – she didn't know anything about keeping a horse, and surely she would need more skills than she currently possessed. Looking after a horse was such a huge responsibility and, really, she did not know an awful lot about them. She couldn't wait to continue the conversation.

However, Daisy took her mind off the subject once they were out on the hill. It was very windy and conversation was difficult. The wind blew the words away the minute they were uttered, so shouting and hand signals were the order of the day. Daisy had had a few days off after the charity ride and was in a very lively mood; it was quite a challenge for Jenny to hold her back before their first canter. Knowing that Daisy was in high spirits, Tina had chosen a route they knew well, and their first canter took them around the edge of an enormous field which was still full of cereal crop. When Jenny had cantered it in previous weeks on Billie's hack, some of the horses had slowed down considerably towards the end, including Daisy. Today though was different, and Daisy was still cantering faster than Jenny would have liked when they were halfway along the fourth side. Tina kept pace with her and held Missy just a head behind Daisy so that she was in the lead, just in case she decided to race.

"Are you OK?" yelled Tina against the wind. "Don't worry, if we have to, we can go round a second time."

It wasn't necessary though, as Daisy pulled up far more easily than Jenny had thought she would and seemed completely satisfied from the release of her pent-up energy. The girls were able to walk back to the yard at a leisurely pace, and on the way they chatted about Jenny having Daisy on a loan arrangement. Tina suggested that Jenny spend all day on Saturday helping at the yard so that she could have some practice at mucking out the stables, turning horses out into the paddocks and bringing others in to be ridden.

***

Jenny thoroughly enjoyed working at the yard on the Saturday. She asked a lot of questions, learned a great deal and relished the idea of being at the yard every weekend in the future to do the same things for Daisy. By the end of the day Wendy had written out a contract for her to sign with a list of things which from now on would be her responsibility.

On the way home Jenny stopped at the tack shop and bought a book on the care of horses, some meadow-herb flavoured horse treats and a small purple tack box which contained some samples of basic grooming equipment. The tack shop sold everything you could think of for both horse and rider and she had always loved browsing the shelves. Now she had a real reason to buy these things for herself! She could hardly believe it. There was a lovely display of colourful horse rugs and saddlecloths in the shop window and she resolved to buy a new saddlecloth for Daisy as soon as she could – she would embroider Daisy's name upon it.

Wendy had assured Jenny that she and the staff would always be on hand to help and to answer questions, and she had said to her, "Always remember, Jenny, that riding is only a very small part of having a horse – 90% of your time is spent on the ground and around the stable. That is where your relationship is made or broken, and a good relationship on the ground means a good relationship in the saddle."

This made a great deal of sense to Jenny, although it was not something she had really thought about before. As a result, she decided that for her first day she would arrive at the yard very early to bring Daisy in for her breakfast and – since Tina had said it was one of Daisy's favourite things – she would give her a bath and wash her mane and tail using some of the grooming products in her new tack box. Tina had given her a 'Good Luck' card and a new purple head collar and lead rope as a present, and this seemed the perfect day to use it for the first time. Jenny felt very nervous entering the mares' paddock on her own for the first time. Daisy was as far away from the gate as she could possibly be and Jenny had to walk through all the others to get to her. They all seemed much bigger than they looked in their stables and most of them had their heads down and were grazing, but Jenny was concerned that any of them could kick out at her if they were suddenly startled and she began to feel nervous. Daisy was standing with her back to the fence and her eyes closed.

Chapter Fourteen

A New Beginning

"Wake up, Daisy, it's our first day together!" Jenny said as soon as she reached her.

Daisy didn't move as Jenny slipped the new head collar over her ears, clipped the rope under her chin and began to walk back to the gate. She could feel Daisy's unease immediately, although she couldn't really say how, she just knew that Daisy was uneasy. It seemed to her that it was because Daisy was not free to defend them both if any of the other mares came too close to them or kicked out at them, so Jenny promptly unclipped the lead rope and to her delight Daisy continued to walk by her side without it. As they approached the gate, Jenny could see two mares, one on each side of the gate, blocking their exit. They both had their heads over the gate and their bottoms facing the paddock, and Jenny thought that if she and Daisy got too close they could be kicked. When they were about seven metres away, Daisy stopped and lifted her head as if she had only just noticed them.

Jenny said to her, "We'll have to deal with it between us, Daisy. You move the one on the right and I'll move the one on the left."

Jenny somehow instinctively knew that Daisy would understand her, and she was absolutely right – as they continued towards the gate, Daisy trotted towards the mare on the right and shooed her away by extending her neck and tossing her head. This gave Jenny better access to the mare on the left and she clapped her hands to shoo her away as well. Daisy then trotted around in an arc to the right and came straight back to the latch end of the gate, arriving at exactly the same time as Jenny, who clipped the rope under her chin again and they were through the gate and in the lane in a trice. She gave Daisy a good rub on her neck.

"Teamwork, Daisy!" she said, feeling very pleased that they were able to work together so easily – and on the very first occasion she had ever brought Daisy in without someone else accompanying her! *What a very good start*, she thought to herself as they walked back to the yard.

Bath time was enormous fun. Daisy seemed to thoroughly enjoy the warm soapy water and the feeling of the sponge on her back. Her mane was a little tricky to rinse as Jenny was very careful not to get soap or water in Daisy's eyes, so instead the water from the hose ran down Jenny's arms. She was also totally unprepared for Daisy shaking when she was covered in foamy shampoo, so by the time they had finished both shampoo and rinse Jenny was absolutely soaked. Once she had used her new rubber scraper to remove the surplus water, as Tina had shown her, she threw a very large bath towel over Daisy's back to dry her off a little while she sorted out the tangle in Daisy's very long thick tail. Eventually she was able to stand back and admire her handiwork and was very pleased with how clean and shiny Daisy now looked.

The stable was already freshly mucked out for them. Once Daisy had wolfed down the contents of her rubber feed bowl, she pushed the bowl around the stable with her nose as if that would magically refill it again. Then she made a beeline for her pile of hay and began to spread it around the edges of her stable while Jenny went off to have a well-earned coffee and biscuits. By the time she returned, Daisy was once again intently watching the activity around the yard with her head hanging over her door. As Jenny approached, Daisy nickered to her expectantly.

"How are you getting on?" asked Wendy, walking past them with a saddle in her arms.

"So far so good," replied Jenny. "I was just wondering what to do next actually. I don't feel confident enough to hack out on my own yet and it seems a shame to finish for the day now."

"Why not use one of the empty outdoor schools?" suggested Wendy. "There are plenty of people about if you have a problem. You could practise some walking and trotting, stopping and starting, backing up and turning. There are some coloured blocks and poles in the school nearest the office; you could have a play with weaving in and out of them in a figure of eight."

Jenny thought this seemed like a very good idea and went off to the school to lay out some of the equipment before going to tack Daisy up. It seemed very odd, leading Daisy out of her stable and into the school all on her own, and it seemed even more strange not being given instructions by a teacher. She found it quite difficult having to decide what to do for herself. After a while though, she got the hang of it and was careful to change the rein for each exercise and change direction too to make it more interesting for Daisy. Sue had once said to her, "She's a bright little mare, Jenny; always keep her thinking and listening to you because if you stop communicating with her and she has an empty head she will fill it with something of her choice and not yours."

After about thirty minutes Jenny had run out of ideas and she thought they may as well finish on a good note, so they left the school and she took Daisy back to her stable. Once she had untacked her and turned her out again, Jenny went off to the tack room to clean all the tack. Karen was there, busily cleaning all the pony saddles, and Jenny spent a pleasant hour chatting to her.

Jenny and Tina had made their usual booking for the following Thursday morning and had decided that Tina would show Jenny two of the shorter one-hour rides, which Jenny might begin with, when she was ready to hack out on her own. Both rides had the benefit of being close to the village and neither offered any opportunity for a canter, so there would be no danger of Daisy taking off with her. The two rides were popular in bad weather, or were used when a horse had been off work with injury and was being brought back to fitness. Sometimes they were used for novices who had not yet learned to canter. In theory, Jenny knew that the rider decided what the horse was going to do, but in practice, when the rider was still learning and quite inexperienced, the less temptation a mischievous horse had the better!

The first ride only took them about forty-five minutes and was basically a loop around the lanes from the yard to the village church and back again a different way. Towards the end of it, Tina showed Jenny a field adjacent to the lane where there was a gate which took you onto the canal path, from which, after about 200 metres, you could go through another gate onto a field which ran parallel to the canal. This offered an opportunity for a short canter back down the field to the lane again. This ride was, she said, generally used by staff who were exercising the livery horses during the winter. The second ride was in the opposite direction and consisted of a sandy track which skirted the wood before joining a tarmac lane and passing a large organic farm where a very picturesque farmhouse was set back from the road behind a beautiful cottage garden.

Jenny already knew four of Daisy's favourite things, namely: dandelions, galloping about, jumping and being bathed. Until now, she was not aware of anything which Daisy *didn't* like. She had seemed remarkably brave helping the other horses to go past the roadworks during Billie's hack; she was not frightened by the hot-air balloon when Jenny fell off, or the iron bath in the woods which they had seen on the charity ride. However, as they were walking past the farmhouse and marvelling at how picturesque the garden was, Daisy suddenly put her head down and ran backwards, before spinning 180 degrees and cantering off up the road and back to where they had come from. As Daisy ducked her head and spun around, Jenny tipped forward and sideways over Daisy's neck and as a result struggled to get upright and balance again during Daisy's canter along the road.

After bumping up and down painfully on the saddle for some distance she was able to right herself and pull Daisy up. Daisy was clearly terrified, her nostrils were flared, and she was breathing heavily and snorting, dancing noisily on the tarmac in her metal shoes. Jenny turned Daisy again to face the direction of the farm as Tina trotted towards them.

"Whatever was all that about?" asked Jenny.

"Pigs!" replied Tina. "Two enormous pigs on the front lawn. I have never seen them before. I had a proper look and they are hidden from view behind the hedge, so she must have smelled them. Shall we have another go? We are only about five minutes from the yard going this way, I don't really want to retrace our steps and, anyway, she should know better!"

They headed towards the farmhouse again and this time didn't even get as far as the garden before Daisy spun and cantered off, but this time Jenny was ready for it and went straight into her half-seat position from which it was easier for her to balance and pull Daisy up. After a failed third attempt they swapped horses and Jenny rode Missy, who didn't seem to mind the pigs at all, but even Tina had great difficulty in getting Daisy past the garden.

"Sorry about that," said Tina when they were almost back at the yard. "What a pity, that is such a useful ride if you don't have a horse which is afraid of pigs! I do know one thing though – we need to work on your sitting canter; we have neglected it since you started hacking. You came within a whisker of falling off back there!"

Chapter Fifteen

Starting Out
Together

Jenny had decided that for the next week she would
visit the yard every day, not always to ride or bring
Daisy in or turn her out, but also just to see her and
say hello and take her a carrot, or to groom her or watch
her being used for lessons in the indoor school. On the
Monday evening, she was at the yard by 6 p.m. as Daisy
was being used for two lessons, one after the other. The
first was with a lady who was just starting to ride and
the whole lesson was spent in walk and was rather dull

to watch, although Jenny was quietly pleased that Daisy was so kind and patient for the lady, who made lots of mistakes. It illustrated for Jenny how riding school horses have to 'know their job' and how they seem to understand when to listen to signals from a competent rider and when to ignore them because the rider cannot ride very well. *It must be very confusing for riding school horses at times*, she thought, and she could see why horses sometimes did what they wanted to do instead of what was asked of them.

The second lesson involved a group of teenagers who were learning to jump and this was much more fun to watch. Jenny realised that Daisy's young rider was Felicity, who had taken Daisy to Summer Camp from which she was sent home in disgrace. Jenny felt a pang of envy at seeing how well Daisy could jump, and how much Felicity enjoyed it too, and resolved to one day learn to jump herself. She remembered that Wendy had told her how at Summer Camp Daisy had taken off around the jumping arena without Felicity, and Jenny could now see first-hand how enthusiastic Daisy was about jumping.

If only Daisy were hers, no-one else would need to ride her unless Jenny asked them to. Tina had told her that many people who bought their own horses later regretted it and that it all ended in tears. This was either because of the cost, or because they did not have enough time to exercise them, or because a great deal of work was necessary to look after a horse every day of the year no matter what the weather. Sometimes, if an owner was unable to exercise the horse often enough and the horse was then too lively, they were frightened by it, which made them even less likely to ride. Lively horses were sometimes difficult to handle and you could potentially end up with an unruly horse. When an owner was desperate to get rid of their horse, the riding school could buy them for a good price. Once the horse was exercised regularly and looked after properly, with a good routine, there was nothing wrong with them.

The following day the weather was fine with only a slight breeze. Tina had said that Daisy shouldn't be too lively after two lessons the previous evening, especially as one was a jumping lesson, and Jenny thought it a perfect opportunity to have a little ride on her own. She decided to try the walk which Tina had shown her, the loop around the lanes from the yard to the village church and back again by a different route. She tacked Daisy up with trembling fingers, and Karen came over to watch her mount up and check that she had tightened the girth properly.

"Do you have your mobile phone with you, Jenny?" she enquired.

"Yes," Jenny replied. "I put the yard telephone number on speed dial just in case!"

Karen reached into her pocket and produced a little card. "Here is my number, just in case you call the yard and the office is empty. I shall be mucking out all morning and will have my phone with me. Don't hesitate to call me if you have a problem."

Jenny nodded and smiled and thought how kind Karen was to be concerned for her.

Jenny's heart thumped loudly as she rode Daisy at walk out of the yard and turned right towards the village. Daisy seemed to be holding back as though she was uncertain, and although she was walking forwards her walk felt a bit sluggish, but Jenny did not like to give her a nudge in case she thought it was a request to change pace. *A slow walk is just fine for the first time out*, thought Jenny to herself.

As they progressed through the village there were people working in their little gardens in front of their houses, trimming bushes, weeding and sweeping the paths. A lady was busy hanging out her washing on a line which was to the side of her garden and at right angles to the road. Jenny was glad that the brightly coloured flapping clothes did not bother Daisy one jot. There was a little boy of about three years of age pushing himself around the garden on a red plastic tractor. He pointed at Daisy as they passed.

"Orsey! Orsey!" he shouted excitedly as he hauled himself off the little tractor and ran to the wooden garden gate. It had no catch upon it and swung open easily as he pulled it towards himself and ran out into the road before his mother could stop him.

She dropped the clothes she was holding back into her washing basket and ran after him, calling, "Matthew! Matthew! Come 'ere!"

Jenny pulled Daisy to a halt and sat rather nervously with her reins as short as she could make them as the little boy stood directly in front of Daisy's knees, hitting her on the leg with one chubby fist. "Orsey! Orsey!" he shouted.

"Matthew!" yelled his mother again as she reached them. "Be nice to the 'orsey!" She rummaged in her pocket and produced the remains of a bag of crisps.

"Give one to the 'orsey, Matthew," she commanded and handed a crisp to the little boy who grasped it between two small fingers and thrust it as high as he could towards Daisy's nose.

Jenny held her breath and at the same time patted Daisy's neck and muttered, "Go gently, Daisy, very gently with the baby."

She had visions of two tiny fingers being bitten off by mistake, or Daisy suddenly moving forward in fright and trampling the child, but she need not have worried – Daisy stood very still and slowly lowered her head and parted her lips to accept the salty morsel. The little boy squealed with delight and, once crisp-free, drew his hand back quickly and pushed it under one armpit, giggling. The sudden noise and speed of his movement startled Jenny, but fortunately not Daisy, who did not move a muscle.

Jenny patted her on the neck again and said to the little boy, "Daisy says thank you, Matthew, thank you very much!"

She raised a hand to touch her riding hat, hoping that the movement would imply that they were about to leave and would encourage Matthew's mother to move him out of their way.

"Say bye bye to the 'orsey," said Matthew's mummy. "Bye bye, 'orsey."

"Bye bye, 'orsey, bye bye, 'orsey," squeaked Matthew as his mother dragged him back by one arm towards the garden gate. Jenny waved them goodbye as she nudged Daisy into walk again and breathed out.

"Gosh, Daisy," she said, "that was scary. Well done for being such a good girl."

Daisy tossed her head up and down as if nodding in agreement and blew down her nose.

As they continued their walk in the sunshine, Jenny began to feel more relaxed and a little more confident. For the first time though, she felt odd; being higher up than everything else made her feel slightly vulnerable, as if she might fall at any moment. In addition, she had not been prepared for the absence of noise which accompanies a lone rider and it reminded her of difficult conversations where everyone stops talking at the same time and no-one quite knows what to say next. The only sound was the rhythmic tap of Daisy's hooves on the road.

The church was a little farther on by a right turn into a lane which took them towards home again. It seemed a good idea to follow the Highway Code and stretch her hand out to the right and ask Daisy to stop. She felt a little silly as there was no-one in front of them or behind – in fact there was no-one else around at all. However, Tina had told her that all good habits start somewhere and, as with children or dogs, being consistent and using the same words and the same signals every time you were in the same situation was the key to good training. It was no different to putting your indicator on in your car to change direction whether there were other cars around or not. As they made the right turn, Daisy's pace quickened and she looked straight ahead until they reached the gate to the canal path, when she looked to her left and slowed down a little.

"Not today, Daisy," Jenny said to her, assuming that she knew about the detour along the canal path and back up the field to the lane. She patted Daisy's neck as she spoke and Daisy nodded again, as if she understood and was agreeing.

"How was she?" asked Tina, who was sitting on the bench outside the office with her sandwich box when they reached the yard.

"Very good," replied Jenny, and she told Tina about Matthew and the crisps.

"They have a dog as well, which rushes out into the road without warning and barks at the horses' heels," said Tina. "Do be aware of that one. Are you hungry, Jenny?" she asked "There are cakes for everyone in the office, my treat."

"Oh, thank you!" said Jenny. "I will just pop Daisy back into her stable for some hay and a rest and then I'll join you."

The office was full of staff when Jenny arrived – Tina had just become engaged to be married! Wendy had asked all the staff to sign a card for her to congratulate her, and she was just about to present this to her and say a few words. Afterwards, Jenny offered her own good wishes and gave Tina a hug. She really valued Tina's kindness and patience and was very grateful for her help with everything. It was nice, she thought, to see her friend so obviously happy and enjoying being the centre of attention. She made a mental note to ask Wendy if there was to be a collection for a gift for Tina and her husband-to-be.

Chapter Sixteen

Carole and Barney

For the next few days, Jenny continued to have a short hack on her own every day, remaining in the paces of walk and trot. She realised that to make it a bit more interesting she could ride each route in reverse, but for the time being she decided to avoid any ride which took her downhill on grass, or any ride where there was flat grass which was normally used for cantering. She did not yet feel able to have a canter on her own as she was worried that Daisy might go too fast or would be difficult to stop. They practised road drill where possible. Jenny always used the same words for the same situations, to be consistent, and she had taken to chatting to Daisy as an antidote to the silence. On one occasion, when they were out of earshot of both the yard and the village, she sang a lively song at a marching tempo and, to her delight, Daisy fell into step in time with the tune! They joined Billie's hack on the Saturday and Billie enquired as to how she was getting on.

"Quite well, I feel," replied Jenny. "I have a list in my head of the next things I need to learn to make further progress, and I can see that gates are really important. I have never had to do them, and I am worried that, if I dismount, Daisy might run away or she may not stand still when I want to get back on again."

"Well, why don't you have a go today?" replied Billie. "It's always better to learn in company as there is always someone to help you out. I quite understand your reasoning; I always do gates from the saddle – it's often a long walk home!"

The first gate they reached was fairly easy to open as they had to push it away from them to go through it. Closing it was another matter! Jenny could now see why it was so important for the rest of the group to stand and face the gate until given the instruction to turn. It was extremely difficult to try and hold the gate and ask Daisy to walk backwards at exactly the right speed at the same time. If Jenny pulled the gate too hard, it banged Daisy's legs and Daisy then walked backwards too quickly to avoid it and Jenny could not reach the gate and had to let go. She began to get flustered because she was taking so long while everyone else was waiting for her.

"Let them wait," said Billie, realising her dilemma. "Take a deep breath and try again. You are nearly there."

After the fourth attempt, although Jenny could feel her cheeks glowing red with embarrassment, she was pleased with their joint achievement and glad that Daisy had been so patient with her.

"Thank you!" she whispered, leaning forward to give Daisy's neck a big pat.

The second gate was much easier as there was a long vertical metal pole which controlled the latch, and the gate itself swung easily on its hinges.

"You will find they are all different," said Billie. "There are gates with stiff catches, gates which you have to lift up to fasten because their hinges have dropped, gates which are difficult to push open and you have to get the horse to push it with their chest. It takes time; you will just have to conquer them gradually. A good horse is a good start, and Daisy isn't just a pretty face, you know, she's very intelligent as well."

Jenny was pleased with Billie's compliment and pleased that the third gate she passed through just needed a bit of a push and it clanged shut of its own accord.

When they returned to the yard, Carole came over to their stable to chat while Jenny was untacking Daisy and preparing to turn her out. "Are you enjoying her?" Carole asked.

"Very much," replied Jenny. "We are just learning to hack out together but sticking to walk and trot at the moment. I cannot imagine feeling confident enough to canter on my own yet, to be honest."

"Well, I haven't had the confidence to go out on my own at all yet," said Carole. "We join in with group hacks and lessons, and I love the indoor school so we use that quite a bit. I was going to ask you if you fancied teaming up for a hack. Beginners together, that sort of thing."

"I'd love to!" said Jenny, lifting Daisy's saddle onto the top of her stable door as she spoke. "When were you thinking of?"

"Tomorrow morning?" suggested Carole. "I can have Barney in from the field and ready for action by around 10 a.m. Would that suit you?"

Jenny readily agreed. She had ridden with Carole several times in lessons and remembered Barney, a polite and well-behaved gelding of about 15.3 hands. He was the most beautiful colour, a sort of pale gold, with a long thick blond mane and tail and two white socks. He was quite stocky and solid, and consequently very powerful, and was popular in the jumping class.

The following morning Carole was already mounted and in the cobbled yard waiting as Jenny led Daisy around.

"Any idea where you might like to go?" Jenny asked Carole.

"I was going to suggest taking the right fork off the chalk track, staying to the right of the copse and following the base of the hill. We can do the whole ride in walk," Carole replied.

"Sounds perfect," said Jenny as she mounted.

As they left the yard, Daisy flattened her ears and tossed her head at Barney, who meekly fell into step about a head behind her.

"Sorry," said Jenny, feeling a bit embarrassed, "she obviously thinks she should be in charge this morning. Are you OK with that?"

"Well, you have had more experience hacking with her than I have with Barney," replied Carole. "It's probably a good idea, to be honest. Poor Barney – outnumbered by the girls this morning!"

They made their way along the chalk track at a leisurely walk, chatting as they did so. Carole told Jenny how she had had her own horse a few years before but had sold him. He had belonged to a friend and had always seemed very well-behaved. The friend was not a particularly good rider, about the same level as Carole, and she thought that since her friend had had no difficulty with the gelding, neither would she. Carole's family did not have enough land for it to live out all year round, and what she had not bargained for was the difference in the animal when it was stabled. It became, she said, an absolute psycho, rearing at the slightest thing, spooking at every fluttering leaf, bolting almost every time she rode it. She had fallen off a few times and it had really ruined her confidence, she said, but nevertheless, she had felt a sense of responsibility and desperately tried to manage it.

The last straw was when it escaped from the paddock, bolted down the road, tried to jump a barbed wire fence and badly cut its leg. The leg had to be stitched and the gelding kept on box rest until it healed, and things went from bad to worse. The farrier had found a new owner for her and had assured Carole that the horse would be well looked after and that she would be able to visit it if she wanted to. She had not ridden again until this year, and Barney was restoring her confidence – that was why she had him on loan.

At the end of the track they took a right turn towards a little copse which was on their left. It was often called 'The Haunted Wood', Carole said, but she did not know why. Just after they passed the trees, the track dipped sharply and descended at a very steep gradient for about fifty metres, before bottoming out and rising just as sharply, upwards again to the base of the hill. As they drew level with the first tree, Daisy gave a little skip and set off at a fast canter, and before she had gone two metres she was galloping flat out downhill. Jenny rose into half-seat and froze; she could do nothing at that speed but remain in position, and she held her breath as they hurtled at top speed down the seemingly vertical track. After another skip from Daisy to change legs, they hurtled up the other side at an equally alarming rate. At the top, Daisy slowed and stopped of her own volition before Jenny even had time to pull her up.

Jenny quickly turned to see where Carole was, terrified that she may have come to some harm, but Barney was still in walk, slowly picking his way down the stony track, and once he was at the bottom he increased his pace a little to walk up the slope towards them.

"Oh my goodness!" said Carole when she reached them. "I don't know what surprised me most, the way she took off without warning, the speed at which she rocketed downhill, the fact that she didn't break either her neck or yours, the fact that you stayed on, or the speed at which she screeched to a halt!"

Jenny was still shaking and could feel tears filling her eyes. She tried very hard to concentrate on keeping her composure.

Carole, sensing the mixture of embarrassment, shock and relief Jenny felt, said kindly, "Ten out of ten, Jenny, well done! I don't know many people who could have ridden that. As for Daisy, she didn't bolt, which she could easily have done – she stopped without being asked and is now waiting patiently for Barney! That was simply high spirits because it's something she likes to do – no harm meant and never any intention to put you at any risk, I'm sure of that. I have never seen anything quite like it, I must admit. That is a very unusual horse you have there."

Jenny smiled a watery smile in response.

"I do hope we can stay in walk now for the rest of the hack!" she said, still feeling wobbly and trying to sound brighter than she felt.

Their journey home was relaxing by comparison but Jenny still felt quite shaky when she put Daisy back in her stable and brushed her off before turning her out. Normally she chatted to Daisy while grooming her but today she worked in silence, not feeling in a very chatty mood. While she was combing Daisy's tail, Daisy turned her head to look at her.

"I don't know whether I am talking to you, Daisy," said Jenny. "You frightened me, you know."

Daisy shook her head from side to side as if in disagreement. Jenny finished grooming and began to pack up the grooming tools, while Daisy turned to her pile of hay and began separating it. As Jenny bent down to pick up the empty breakfast feed bowl and take it out to be washed, Daisy turned with a large mouthful of hay and dropped it on top of Jenny's head.

"Ughhhh!" said Jenny, brushing it off with one hand and blowing it out of her mouth. "What was that for?"

Daisy lifted her head and parted her lips, quivering them upwards. Jenny could not help but laugh – it looked to her as if that was exactly what Daisy was doing.

"It isn't funny, Daisy!" she said, without much conviction, as she was already starting to laugh.

Daisy enthusiastically nodded her head up and down as if she were saying, 'Oh yes it is.'

"I need a coffee," Jenny said to her. In spite of her earlier upset she was beginning to feel brighter. "Try and stay out of mischief until I get back, please!" And she watched as Daisy turned away again to concentrate on her hay.

CHAPTER SEVENTEEN

TEDDY

A few days later, Jenny was in Daisy's stable preparing to turn her out after their ride, when Tina appeared at the door.

"Hi," she said, "how are you both? How are you getting on?"

"Well, thank you," replied Jenny. "Hacking out on my own is getting a little easier. I am trying to extend the distances we go and to learn new routes, by using a known route, then adding just an extra 500 metres or so before turning around and coming home, and the next time we go out as far as the place where we finished on the previous occasion and then ride a bit further before turning around, and so on. I've printed out a map and I mark our routes with yellow highlighter pen so that I remember them."

"It all sounds very well organised!" Tina sounded impressed. "Have you had a canter on your own yet?"

"Err… no," said Jenny hesitantly. "Well, not of my choosing anyway, though we did have a gallop down a chalk track which seemed almost vertical."

"I heard," said Tina, pulling a face. "Well done for staying on! Carole was very impressed."

"It's put me off doing anything but walking, quite frankly," said Jenny. "I haven't even trotted since. I'm not sure what to do next to get my confidence back."

"Ah, confidence," said Tina: "hard won, easily lost. Well, I have three suggestions. Firstly you could have a session in one of the empty outdoor schools, maybe once a week, just to re-visit walk, trot, transitions and even a half-seat canter when you are feeling relaxed. Your balance is really good and I should be very surprised if she played up in school as she can neither go very fast nor very far! I say the outdoor school, as you will not have that feeling of crashing into the end wall; it will seem much more natural to canter in the fresh air. I am happy to stand and watch for your first canter if you think that would help. The second thing is, if you plan to have your first canter out, we can use her for a lesson or some other work before, just to take the edge off her enthusiasm. The third thing is, we have a new horse which one of the clients wants to buy once it has been vetted, and I am personally exercising it every day for the next two weeks. If, for example, you decided to have your first solo canter at The Cutting, I could do my hack in reverse so that I met you at the top halfway round and we could walk home together down the track. That way, you would know you were not completely alone on the hill if you had a problem."

"Gosh, thank you!" said Jenny. "All those things sound very helpful and I shall take your advice. When do you next exercise the new horse? What is his name, by the way?"

"His name is Teddy," said Tina, "which is a pity, as he is the furthest thing from small, fluffy and cuddly you ever saw! I ride him every day about 10 a.m., and I always use the cobbled yard mounting block so that he gets into a routine for his new owner. Come and find me when you feel ready to have a go." And with a grin and a wave she was gone.

The weather was beginning to change and had turned much cooler, especially in the early morning and late afternoon. The horses would not be living out at night for much longer and were now lightly rugged in case it either rained overnight or there was a very early frost. The leaves on the trees were turning gold, orange and cinnamon brown, and the ground felt much softer under both foot and hoof.

After her conversation with Tina, Jenny was determined to regain her confidence as soon as possible, and she decided she would spend half an hour in the outdoor school before each hack in the hope that it would settle Daisy down. It seemed to work very well and Daisy appeared to enjoy it. After a few days, Jenny had regained her confidence in Daisy's rhythmic bouncy trot and one morning felt the urge to try a canter. She nudged Daisy into the transition, rose into half-seat and was so thrilled to ride three laps in perfect balance that her face broke into a broad grin.

"Let's finish on a high note, Daisy!" she said, dismounting and leading Daisy towards the school gate. She looked at her watch, it was 9:50 a.m. – she might just catch Tina on her way out.

The cobbled yard was empty and some of the stable doors were open. Their occupants were shortly to be brought in from the paddocks for their breakfast and each stable had a lovely new clean, sweet-smelling straw bed, a brightly coloured rubber water bucket in one corner and a fluffy pile of fresh hay in the other. Jenny thought how enticing they all looked and how cosy it must be to spend a night in one, with the wooden door firmly shut, warm and dry, while listening to the wind howling or the rain drumming outside. Each stable had a semi-circular bridle hook and a metal pole for a saddle, fitted to the left of the door. Jenny had found them to be incredibly useful when tacking and untacking.

Tina appeared at that moment and Jenny had her first glimpse of Teddy. Tina had been right, Teddy was a seriously classy, glamorous horse. Fully clipped, spotlessly clean, his gleaming mahogany skin shone with good health and his immaculate shining black mane and tail looked as soft as silk. He was about 16.5 hands tall, finely built but muscular, his hooves gleaming with polish, and he placed each one on the cobbles with the utmost deliberation, as if he knew he was being watched and wanted to look as 'cool' as possible. Jenny had never seen quite such an elegant horse in all her life.

"Good heavens," she said to Tina, "he's like a film star! His name should be Armani, not Teddy. However much did he cost?"

"Five figures," replied Tina. "He is a brilliant achiever, as well as being glamorous, dressage mainly. He has had quite an unnatural life, stabled virtually all the time except for exercise in an arena. Hacking is a new experience for him and he finds it quite challenging, I don't think he has ever seen mud in his life. Daisy is honoured to be the first school horse to ride with him, so I do hope she doesn't blot her copy book and let the side down!"

"Are you listening, young lady?" Jenny asked as she leaned over to pat Daisy on the neck. "Best behaviour today, please."

They left the yard together but Tina soon peeled off to the left to climb the hill while Jenny continued along the long straight track towards the fork in the track and The Cutting. To give Daisy something to think about, she practised Scout's pace, fifty metres of walk and fifty metres of trot alternately. They soon reached the little wooden gate which fortunately Jenny found easy to open; she had forgotten that there would be a gate. She had been practising with gates as much as she could, both the gates of empty paddocks around the yard and gates in and out of the outdoor school, as well as gates they found while out hacking. She had kept to the principle of 'stand and face the gate' even when they were on their own once the gate was closed, and on this occasion she was relieved that Daisy was in no hurry to turn around until requested to do so. It gave Jenny a moment to take a deep breath, and she was half expecting Daisy to suddenly take off, but surprisingly she even waited for the command to trot.

After a few paces, Jenny sat in the saddle and nudged Daisy's sides and was rewarded with a lovely smooth transition. Jenny confidently cantered up the hill, and she even felt able to give Daisy a little nudge to pick up the pace to make it easier to balance. Once at the top of the hill they made a lovely smooth downward transition and Jenny leaned forward while still in motion and rubbed Daisy's neck vigorously.

"Well done!" she exclaimed. "What a good girl you are, Daisy!" and she laughed as Daisy nodded her head up and down in agreement.

They made their way back to the track just as Tina came into view further up above them, and Jenny halted Daisy and relaxed her rein while they waited.

"How was it?" called Tina when she was within earshot.

"Textbook perfect!" replied Jenny proudly. "She behaved so beautifully for me. What a star!"

She glanced down at Daisy and noticed that she had lifted her head and neck, almost meerkat-like, thought Jenny, or like a dog which has just seen something interesting and freezes with one paw in the air. She supposed the something interesting must be Teddy.

"I am so pleased for you," said Tina when she was near enough. "You have worked so hard, you deserve a big pat on the back yourself."

As Tina drew near, Jenny gave Daisy a nudge to move forward, but to her surprise Daisy stood still, waited for Teddy to come alongside her and then dropped into step a head behind him.

"Good grief!" said Jenny "I thought boys had to give way to you, Daisy?"

"I do think she's impressed!" said Tina, chuckling. "Our Daisy is deferring to glamour boy here. What a hoot!"

On the way back to the yard Daisy made no attempt to lead, she turned her head to look at Teddy often and the girls were most amused by her unusually courteous demeanour.

"I think she fancies him," said Tina, grinning. "He's out of your league I'm afraid, my lovely. But hey, what a great way to get her to behave herself!"

"Well, I did ask her to be on her best behaviour, perhaps she remembers that," said Jenny, laughing.

Chapter Eighteen

The Mischief-Ometer Reading

O ver the next two months, Jenny and Daisy really expanded their hacking territory. Jenny delighted in printing new maps and, once she had ridden all the tracks and byways and coloured them yellow, she copied the entire map again, so that she had a perfect reference to take with her in her inside jacket pocket. The originals, she pinned onto a cork board which she hung on her bedroom wall. She was therefore able to see at a glance where she might ride next so that she kept up the variety and did not ride the same route too often. She had recently begun to work through the routes again but this time highlighting in bright orange pen any canters they had tried.

The canters were becoming more predictable and, although during this time Daisy began to be stabled each night and was quite lively and eager, the combination of being worked in lessons with clients and a warm-up with Jenny in the outdoor school before each hack seemed to keep Daisy's energy at a manageable level. Tina called it 'The Mischief-ometer' reading. Jenny found that the canters often started as if they were about to compete in the Grand National, but then settled almost instantly into a reasonable measured pace, and Jenny had, thankfully, not once had difficulty in getting Daisy to pull up. She was learning to trust Daisy and hoped that the reverse was true. She talked to Daisy a great deal when they were on their own.

They had joined some group hacks with Billie on Saturdays, and Billie had suggested that Jenny ride more independently of the group. For example, when Billie asked everyone to trot, Jenny would ask Daisy to remain in walk instead and then, after a few paces, she gave the command to trot. Or she would ask her to halt and wait when the whole ride was trotting away and then ask her to trot after she had stood nicely for a few minutes. In this way, Billie explained, Daisy would realise that she was not always doing the job of a riding school pony when she was out in a group.

Billie had had a long conversation with Jenny, which Jenny had found fascinating. It was one very wet afternoon when Billie had finished work but was waiting for the farrier to arrive for her own horse, Cara. One of the things she said was that horses, by and large, feel very responsible for their riders and would hate to have them fall off or be hurt. They also have their own great sense of self-preservation, and often, if they balk at something frightening or want to flee, it is actually a very sensible reaction and one without which they would not have survived for over a million years.

Billie reminded Jenny of the incident with the road menders, when Cara had thought it too risky to continue, and in order to protect herself and the group she had refused to pass. There is a distinction, Billie said, between overruling your horse and insisting that it does something which it is afraid of because you know it's safe; and assuming it is being silly just because you cannot smell the rather angry bull which is in the field you are about to walk through. Horses are not stupid, she said, and have keen eyes to spot the dangerous barbed wire lurking in the long grass. It is a good thing to know your horse and to know when to insist it does as you say, and equally when to respect its caution and hold back and check. Many a rider, said Billie, has assumed their superiority and later regretted it.

The weather became more unpredictable and the days became shorter. The bedraggled autumn leaves gradually fell from the trees and skulked around the gutters in untidy groups, they swirled around Daisy's hooves and chased her up the lanes. Jenny had ridden in the rain when it was fairly light rain, but had used an exercise sheet of Tina's which kept not only the saddle but also Daisy's rump nice and dry. On days when it was raining too heavily to venture out, Jenny had rugged Daisy up and turned her out for some extra free time in the paddock to give her a change of scenery and let her mingle with the other mares. Meanwhile, Jenny mucked out the stable and cleaned tack, chatted to the other girls or watched lessons taking place in the indoor school.

It was not really necessary for her to do these chores like mucking out, but she really enjoyed working out in the fresh air and loved the atmosphere around the yard. On such wet days, Jenny would towel Daisy off after bringing her in and before putting on her stable rug. And she discovered that Daisy had a liking for black tea. Jenny realised this when Daisy's tongue had expressed too much interest in Jenny's cup, and Jenny, fearful that her friend might burn her tongue, had poured some tea into her cupped hand and was amused when Daisy had lapped it up with great enthusiasm, before lifting her head and parting her lips, presumably to show that she liked the taste. Tea was often accompanied by the sharing of an apple, cut into eight pieces. Daisy was a very polite sharer and did not nudge Jenny's hand or try to scoff more apple than her fair share.

Chapter Nineteen

Daisy has Something to Say

To Jenny's amusement, Daisy was, in her own way, beginning to express her opinion about things. On one occasion they had been out for a hack and Jenny was preparing to turn Daisy out into the paddock. It was grey and overcast and, when Jenny approached Daisy with her outdoor rug, Daisy shook her head from side to side and turned away. Jenny went round to the other side of her and gave her a pat and attempted to put the rug on again, but again Daisy shook her head from side to side as if to say no, and this time turned her back so that her rump was facing Jenny. So Jenny went around to Daisy's head, scratched her neck gently with her fingers and said, "Don't you want to go out with the others?"

Daisy shook her head from side to side again.

"OK," said Jenny. "Well, it's an early night for you, then! I'll put your stable rug on instead and get some more hay."

As she fastened the straps on the rug, there was an almighty cracking sound and a loud bang, as an enormous flash of lightning lit up the sky and there was a tremendous rumble.

"Mmm, good call, Daisy," said Jenny, realising that Daisy had sensed the forthcoming storm and had not wanted to get wet. "We both would have been really soaked before we'd even got you to the paddock."

Jenny did not like the idea of going out in the rain either, so she remained in the stable for a while and stood at the door, watching the sudden frantic activity as girls ran around closing doors to stop them from being broken off their hinges by the sudden gale blowing through the yard. It was cosy in the stable and the fresh smell of the sudden heavy rain mingled with the sweet fragrances of hay and straw.

On another occasion, Jenny was riding a route she had only ridden once before and the turning she expected to see was not as she remembered it. She pulled Daisy up, gave her a pat and said, "Just a minute, I need to look at the map."

She fished it out of her pocket to study it and, sure enough, the yellow highlighted pen marked a turn to the left, even though it seemed unfamiliar to her.

"OK, Daisy, left it is," she said and proceeded to open Daisy's left rein a little and nudge her with her right foot. Daisy remained where she was, turned her head to the right and nodded her head up and down vigorously. *Heavens*, thought Jenny, giggling, *now she is arguing*!

"Please, pretty please, Daisy, may we turn left?" Jenny said with mock deference.

She opened her rein slightly and put a little pressure on Daisy's right side with her foot a second time. Daisy didn't move her feet at all; instead, she turned her head to the right and nodded it up and down vigorously again.

"Daisy!" said Jenny, as firmly as she could without wishing to sound cross. "Please! We are turning left."

This time, Daisy listened to Jenny's signal and obligingly turned to the left. They had not gone very far before Jenny realised that she did not recognise this part of the ride at all. This track took them into a wood with a grass path, other grass paths criss-crossed the one they were on and there was a small fallen tree to one side of the track. Jenny was quite sure she had not seen it before. She was just thinking that perhaps she had made a mistake and was wondering whether they should in fact turn around and go back, when Daisy halted abruptly and with two skips turned a full 180 degrees to go back the way they had come. Jenny burst out laughing, leaned over and gave the side of Daisy's neck a good pat and a rub.

"OK, you were right," she said, giggling.

She kept thinking about it and chuckled all the way back to the yard.

Not long afterwards, Jenny was becoming more adventurous and decided to try a completely new route. There was a very wide byway on her map which connected two routes she had previously ridden and it was accessed by a small wood. It was a lovely sunny day, although quite cold with a stiff breeze. The trees had lost virtually all their leaves by now and these were scattered all over the edges of the fields in soggy dark brown piles, as it had rained a great deal over the previous two weeks. Some of the field edges were too muddy to ride where there had been a lot of activity from horses and dog-walkers, so Jenny had to make slight detours to avoid the muddiest parts. The small wood, when they arrived, was fun to walk through, and the thin tracks within it were well trodden and surprisingly dry considering all the rain there had been. It was also sheltered from the wind, and Jenny sang as they walked along, choosing a song which was the same tempo as Daisy's walk, just for fun. There was the occasional boggy patch which Jenny encouraged Daisy to jump across, and upon leaving the wood they walked up the side of the field before joining the byway, which was enclosed on both sides by trees and bushes. It was about the size of a large avenue, thought Jenny, and would have looked very pretty in the summer. There was evidence that off-roaders had used the byway – there were deep ruts in places, some of them filled with muddy water, and occasionally the entire width of the avenue was like a river with thin mudbanks rising up from the water level at the edges of the ruts.

Jenny and Daisy stayed to the right of the avenue, near to the bushes and trees where there was a reasonably wide verge still covered in grass, presumably because it was too close to the trees and the overhanging branches for the drivers. Suddenly, with no warning at all, Jenny felt that they were falling, and a wall of muddy water splashed up all around her. Equally suddenly she felt herself being thrown back upwards again, and Daisy stopped abruptly and stood still, breathing heavily. Jenny looked down and around her – they were on a small piece of grass at the right of the avenue, Daisy was covered all over in thick muddy water, which was dripping from her coat and mane, and Jenny's legs and boots were soaked too. She looked around and noticed that the rut behind them looked much like the others to her left. With alarm, she realised they had fallen into some sort of deep hole; perhaps the ground had even given way beneath them, she knew not, although they had been very careful to remain on the grass verge. Daisy's quick reaction had been to jump upwards again immediately she felt herself falling, and fortunately she had managed to get them out. Jenny could see that they were standing on a tiny island of mud, very close to thorn bushes on their right, with muddy water swirling horribly close to their left. She kept very still but dropped her right hand onto Daisy's neck.

"Good girly," she said. "Thank you, well done. You have to be very, very good for a moment while I think about what is best to do." She realised to her dismay that they might not have long. The ground they were standing on might also collapse beneath their weight and, although she was almost too frightened to move, they had to do something. She patted Daisy again. Looking around her, she could see there was only one solution. There were small gaps between the thorn bushes on their right, some of the bushes were fairly spindly, and Jenny thought the tiny branches would break if they forced their way through. Being scratched and bleeding was far preferable to getting stuck in thick deep mud and being unable to get out. It was a terrifying thought.

"To the right, girly. We need to push our way through the gaps between those bushes, then we can get back into the field," Jenny said, indicating right with her rein and giving Daisy a tiny nudge with her left foot.

Daisy remained motionless, except to turn her head to the left and nod it up and down vigorously. "We can't, Daisy. It's too dangerous to go to the left," Jenny said to her. "I don't know how deep those ruts are, and if you get stuck in one I can't get you out."

Her heart began to pound and, again, she gave Daisy the signal to push through the bushes on their right.

"Go on, Daisy!" she said. "Go on!" She kicked with both feet as she spoke, to try to urge Daisy to respond. Again, Daisy remained motionless, except to turn her head to the left and nod it up and down vigorously.

Oh help, thought Jenny, *how on earth can I make her understand that we can't possibly cross all those ruts? Whatever is she thinking of?*

Twice more she asked Daisy to turn to the right and twice more Daisy remained rooted to the spot, apart from turning her head to the left and nodding, the last time even more vigorously, as if she too felt the need to move urgently and was becoming exasperated at Jenny's hesitance. Jenny looked down and noticed that the mud they were standing on was now completely covering Daisy's hooves. They were gradually sinking! Jenny felt panic rising within her; she knew they needed to move and move quickly. Billie's voice popped into her head at that moment: *You need to know when to insist and when to respect their caution.*

Well, this wasn't so much caution as a simple difference of opinion, Jenny thought... but Daisy had been right last time... She wasn't a stupid animal, far from it. She wasn't making a fuss, rearing or bolting, she was standing quite calmly, waiting, waiting for the signal to take the route she clearly thought was best.

Know when to insist and when to respect, again Jenny remembered Billie's words; *many a rider has regretted assuming their superiority.*

Billie had made no mention of the horse insisting something, of course – was this usual? wondered Jenny. Is this what horses do? She had never known a dog to behave like this. With a sigh she realised that she actually had no choice, she dare not delay any longer. She patted Daisy's neck.

"OK, Daisy, you win," she said, as she loosened her rein to the buckle so that Daisy was free to stretch as much as she needed to. At the same time, Jenny checked her own position and held on tightly to the front of her saddle with both hands. Daisy turned to her left and immediately jumped across the nearest rut, and with two more jumps she had cleared the waterlogged avenue and they were in the field, standing safely on the grass. Jenny looked back at where they had come from – it seemed a considerable distance, maybe ten or twelve metres, and Daisy must have jumped from rut edge to rut edge to get them across. Jenny leaned forward and made a huge fuss of Daisy; she felt emotional with relief, thankful and very humble that she had the good fortune to have such an intelligent and capable animal as her friend.

"I think this is definitely a day when I donate my half of the apple to you, Daisy," she said, and she turned Daisy to the left so that they could retrace their steps through the quiet little wood and make their way home the way they had come.

Chapter Twenty

The Farrier and the Carrots

Back at the yard, Jenny had to fetch some warm water to wash the mud off Daisy. The water from the hosepipe was icy and generally too cold to give her a proper bath, and sponging off the worst of the mud with warm water was the best she could do in the circumstances. Tina came over to them as Jenny was working quickly with a sponge, not wanting Daisy to stand too long in the cold after her ride.

"Whatever happened to you two?" asked Tina,

looking bemused. "You look as if you've been swimming in a muddy river."

"We almost were!" said Jenny, smiling, and she told Tina all about their mishap.

"Crikey!" said Tina. "Gosh, you were lucky. You sometimes read in the papers about horses and ponies getting stuck in holes and the fire brigade having to pull them out. I will mention it to Wendy – there should be a sign along there to indicate 'No Entry' or something if it's that unsafe for walkers and riders." Tina shuddered at the thought of what might have happened.

"I actually came to tell you that the farrier is here and Daisy is on his list. If you can towel her off as much as possible I will bring you a microfibre rug to pop on her so she doesn't get cold and catch a chill standing about damp on such a cold day, then perhaps you can bring her round to the back yard?"

The back yard was very quiet as the only horses kept there were on box rest, usually because they were recovering from injury or illness. There was a large rug room in the back yard and a drying room which contained the washing machine, where all the saddlecloths, girths and rugs were laundered, plus two rug dryers. The feed room was also in the back yard; it contained all the different types of horse feeds and various supplements which some of the horses had to have. Jenny always thought the smell in the feed room was really enticing – the sugar beet was soaked there and there was a wonderful aroma of dark molasses. Polly was in charge of the feed room and no-one was allowed to take any feed without permission. Once, one of the children had taken a scoop full of part-soaked beet and fed it to her pony as a treat. The beet swelled up inside the pony's stomach and he was very ill and nearly died of colic.

Polly had a friend called Nancy who worked for a catering company in a nearby town, but she lived in the village. Most days, Nancy would call in with a big tub of carrot peelings on her way home and each horse would have a handful in their feed bowl at teatime. Today, the large orange rubber bucket of carrot peelings was already outside the feed room door, ready to be put away.

Jenny walked Daisy round to the back yard. Tom was already there, finishing off one of the hunters, a big grey horse called Max. Tom was a tall man of about thirty years of age, with broad shoulders, jet black hair and tanned skin. His bare arms were tattooed and he wore heavy leather boots and a leather apron with large pockets at the front. He was always cheerful and chatted as he worked, and the horses were very relaxed in his company. If ever a horse was nervous about being shod, perhaps when it was new to the yard, half an hour with Tom usually convinced it that there was nothing to worry about.

Jenny had once watched in fascination as a new and very skittish pony, which spooked at everything and everyone and was incredibly nervous, met Tom for the first time. There was only one entrance to the back yard and there was a chain which stretched across the entrance in place of a gate. On this occasion, Tom had fastened the chain and let the new pony, called Butter, walk about freely with its lead rope dangling over its withers. Halfway through Tom completing the first hoof, the pony had snatched its leg away and quickly trotted off. Tom had let it go without resistance and, after talking to it calmly from across the yard, he approached it again, gave it a lovely rub behind its wither and picked up the leg once more. Gradually, the pony relaxed, and by the time Tom was working on the third and fourth hooves it was happy to stand still without being held or tied up, and it behaved for him beautifully. Tom handed the hunter he had finished to one of the yard girls to take away and looked up as Jenny and Daisy approached.

"Ah! It's Miss Daisy! Hi Daze! How are you today?"

Tom gave her a good scratch to the side of one ear and Daisy tilted her head a little in obvious pleasure. Jenny handed Tom the lead rope and he let it fall to the floor. He walked towards Daisy's tail and ran his hand along her back, over her rump and down a hind leg as she stood perfectly still for him. Jenny noted that he had his back to Daisy's head, and with the words, "Up you go, girly!" he lifted her first hind leg up between his knees to remove its shoe.

Tom chatted to Jenny while he worked; he was full of funny stories about his childhood growing up on a race yard, where his father worked as a trainer, and he had loved horses from even before he could walk. Having removed Daisy's first shoe, Tom dropped her leg and turned away to pick up a different tool and, as he moved, Daisy took three steps backwards and pivoted 180 degrees so that she was facing in the opposite direction, with her head furthest away from him.

"What was that for, Daze?" Tom asked, lifting his old canvas bag of tools and placing it near to her second hind leg.

He continued to work on her as she stood on three feet and, once he let the second leg drop and she had all four feet on the ground again, Daisy walked forwards three paces. Tom kicked his bag along the floor, moved towards her shoulder, picked up a front leg and continued his work without complaint. When he let go of the first foreleg and Daisy had all her feet on the ground again, she stepped forward four paces, further away from Tom.

Yet again he obligingly moved his tool bag.

"What's up, girly? Good job I only have one more to do. You know better than this, my girl, you usually stand like a statue for me."

Jenny watched with amusement. She was not quite sure, but she thought she knew what Daisy was up to and was curious to see what happened next.

Tom let go of Daisy when it was time to heat up the first shoe and, while he was working it with his hammer on the anvil, Daisy walked forward another three paces. Jenny could see that she had perfectly manoeuvred herself into the best position to be able to now drop her head directly into the bucket of carrot peelings outside the feed room door. Jenny promptly burst out laughing and Tom looked up to see what she was laughing at, then shook his head and chuckled.

"Crafty little madam!" he said. "She planned that, she did! No wonder she's been moving about, she wanted to get to the carrots! You're a one, Miss Daisy, that you are."

"Come on, Daisy," said Jenny, going over to Daisy and lifting her head out of the bucket with some difficulty. "Back to Tom, if you please. Shall I hold her for you, Tom?"

"If you wouldn't mind, miss, yes please. I'm not half as interesting as a bucket full of carrot peel."

Tom managed to finish his work without further delay and Jenny led Daisy back to her stable.

"I have to go now," she said to Daisy as she led her into the stable, turned her in a circle, brought her head back towards the door and took the head collar off. She put her arms around Daisy's neck and gave her a hug.

"You're amazing, Daisy," she said. "I am so lucky to have a friend like you. Thank you for looking after us today."

Daisy watched intently while Jenny left the stable and pulled the big bolt across the door from the outside. She rushed across the stable, put her head over the door and made her usual nickering sound. Jenny grinned at her and ruffled her mane.

"Is that a cheerio, Daisy?" she asked with a grin. Daisy nodded her head up and down vigorously and Jenny laughed.

"See you tomorrow, girly," said Jenny as she left.

Chapter Twenty-One

Tina Names the Day

Tina was in the office manning the desk and answering the telephone and she looked up as Jenny entered.

"Are there any biscuits?" Jenny asked her. "I'm famished."

As Tina thrust the biscuit tin across the desk with one hand, the telephone rang and she answered it. The call ended just as Jenny was about to sit down with her coffee.

"I have some news!" Tina said to her, beaming. "We've set the date for our wedding!"

"Congratulations!" said Jenny delightedly. "I am really pleased for you. When is it going to be?"

"It will be the first Saturday in January," said Tina. "Adrian has to take over his cousin's farm in the new year but he wasn't expecting to have to do that so soon, hence the rush. I have to go with him, obviously. There will be so much to organise and I have to give a month's notice here, so we had to make it public straight away."

"You're leaving," said Jenny, feeling a sudden pang of sadness and knowing she must ignore it for Tina's sake.

"Yes, it's very sad," said Tina, looking a little downcast. "I have been so happy here. I've worked here for seven years. But, Jenny, there is ample space on the farm for me to start my own livery yard, and the setting is perfect! Adrian is all for it – diversification in farming is the way to go these days. I am so excited!"

Tina chatted happily about the plans for the wedding and the move. Jenny nodded and smiled as she listened. She was really happy for Tina and glad that the future looked so bright for her, but she felt a little sad at the thought of Tina no longer being around the yard.

After a while she said, "Well, I had better get going. I am longing for a hot shower and to get out of these wet things."

"Of course," said Tina, smiling. "You must, you'll catch your death in this weather." She turned back to the desk then looked up again as Jenny reached the door.

"You will come, won't you, to the wedding?"

Jenny grinned. "Wild horses wouldn't stop me," she said as she left the office.

The following day, Daisy seemed none the worse for their escapade, and Jenny gave her a really good brush to remove any traces of mud she might have missed the day before. All the horses were spending a lot more time in their stables now. It was dark by 4 p.m. and turnout was often limited to just two hours, as the paddocks were beginning to be churned up. Horses which had, for a variety of reasons, not been exercised often enough, ran around the paddocks to let off steam and made the ground even worse, and the grass had stopped growing weeks before, so there could be no recovery until the spring. The gateways were particularly muddy, and on some very wet days paddocks were completely out of bounds and all the horses had to remain in their stables. Daisy became increasingly lively on their hacks, especially if it was windy up on the hills. Jenny had had some hair-raising moments coping with gates and now had to aim for two good canters per hack plus a fair amount of trotting to keep Daisy satisfied. Jenny was often nervous about their first canter and was always relieved to get it out of the way as the second was – usually – less lively.

She had put in some practice at sitting canter as often as she could, but the minute Daisy took off she had no choice but to get into her jockey position straight away. It was now second nature to her and felt absolutely right and very secure, and on the odd occasion Daisy jumped a bush whilst in canter, Jenny didn't move a muscle. Jumping lessons were still on her 'to do' list but until then Daisy took care of the jumping and Jenny just stayed put.

Daisy had developed what Jenny described to Tina as a 'strut'. It was a cross between a very slow trot and a bounce. When Daisy was full of beans and could barely contain her enthusiasm to hooley about, she did not take off with Jenny but instead strutted, raising and lowering her feet at half her normal speed. It was incredibly difficult at first to stay in the saddle in a sitting position, and the only way to stop the 'strut' was to trot. That became quite tiring on occasion and hacks were certainly not as relaxing anymore as Jenny had to concentrate the whole time. In spite of the challenges, she enjoyed hacking immensely and loved every second of every moment she spent with Daisy. However, she was always rather relieved to get both of them back to the yard unharmed.

The south-westerly winds which brought the rains moved on, and the following week was bitterly cold instead. The change was quite a shock but it was much easier, thought Jenny, to keep warm than to keep dry. During the wet weather, she had been using a tiny bit of space on the rug dryer at the yard to dry her coat every day before she left to go home. Hacking in the cold weather was something new and Jenny had asked Tina if it was still OK to hack Daisy out in such cold weather. Tina had said that keeping Daisy's back warm was a priority and suggested they borrow an old exercise rug of hers – it was of a soft fleecy material with a breathable waterproof outer and, although a bit big for Daisy, it was better than her back being cold. Riding school horses did not often need exercise sheets, as hacking was not as popular in very cold weather, Tina had said, but most of the owners had a variety of rugs and sheets and other equipment to keep their horses as comfortable as possible so that they could ride whatever the weather.

Jenny resolved to buy an exercise sheet like Tina's as a Christmas present for Daisy. She spent an hour in the tack shop on the way home and was thrilled with her purchase, a navy blue fleece-lined exercise sheet which fastened over Daisy's withers and was cut to fit underneath the flaps of her saddle. Jenny couldn't wait to try it out but decided to wait until after Christmas Day itself, not that Daisy would have known any different of course, but it just seemed the right thing to do!

CHAPTER TWENTY-TWO

FROST ON THE HILL

The temperatures dropped further and every day seemed a little colder than the last. Frost hung around all day, and even a late and very watery sun in the early afternoon could not make the brittle grass thaw out. The landscape looked delightfully picturesque, but keeping the horses well cared for became more difficult for everyone. The girls were forever changing water buckets as the water in the stables froze so quickly, and the hosepipe had to be removed from the tap every night lest the water in it froze and it could not be used the next morning.

Fortunately, Jenny kept her car in the garage and it started every morning first time. She had ridden Daisy in the indoor school every day for the past four days and had even let her play at liberty over the jumps while she herself stood and watched, but she knew that Daisy, like her, was missing the freedom and variety of hacking out and as a result was fidgety and restless in the stable, rushing to her stable door to look out the minute she heard any noise, such as the movement of horses' hooves on the cobbles.

Wendy was in the office when Jenny went in to warm up one morning and enjoy a cup of hot chocolate.

"We are desperate to hack," she said to Wendy. "School is becoming a bit boring for both of us and I'm beginning to run out of ideas to make it more interesting. Daisy is really fidgety today. I wonder how long this cold spell will last."

"Lots of people have cancelled their lessons in school because of the weather," replied Wendy. "It's just too cold to ride, and all the horses are a bit wired as they are neither having their normal workload, nor their routine turnout. They get bored very quickly in the paddock as they can't graze normally, and hay is not as interesting when you have a pile of it back in your stable. If they get too bored, they run around on frozen ground, which is not good for their legs. Have you thought of just taking her for a good walk up the hill? The thing to avoid is icy ground, like ice on tarmac for example, or frozen water, as she can slip and really hurt herself, but if you can keep to grass everywhere and tread very carefully you may be able to go for a good walk – at least it will be a change of scenery. She will need an exercise sheet though. You might be able to borrow one."

"Tina has lent us hers," replied Jenny. "I've bought Daisy a new one for Christmas! I can't wait to use it but don't want to do that until Boxing Day, when I thought we could have a special ride."

Wendy's face clouded over and she looked as if she was about to say something else, but just at that moment the telephone rang. Jenny finished her drink and left the office to go and tack Daisy up.

As they left the yard and headed out under the bare lime trees, their breath hung in the air. Jenny reached down and put a hand on Daisy's neck; it felt lovely and warm, even through Jenny's leather glove.

"You have to be very good today, Daisy," she said to her. "No hooleying about and no mischief whatsoever. This is just a walk. OK?"

Daisy was busily looking around, as if seeing the landscape for the first time. *It certainly looked different*, thought Jenny. Frozen leaves, which had so far managed to stay on their branches in spite of recent strong winds, now dropped quietly from the trees as they passed.

The birds had stopped singing and there was no colour to be seen anywhere, just a sea of white and pale grey, under a light grey sky. As they made their way up the track, Jenny kept Daisy at a brisk walking pace, until they reached The Cutting when she nudged her into a trot. The rough grass was thick there and not as frozen because it was more sheltered in the 'V' of the hill. It was harder for Daisy to trot up the hill than canter, and at the top Daisy blew down her nose and shook her head a few times. "Hopefully that got rid of some cobwebs, Daisy," Jenny said to her.

At the top, instead of rejoining the track to retrace their steps, they climbed even higher and, as the temperature around them dropped sharply, Jenny felt as if they were ascending into a freezing cloud which obscured the view of everything above and below them. The top of the hill consisted of a large expanse of open ground; it was occupied by sheep at other times of the year, but for now it was quite empty and shrouded in a very light pale mist of frozen air. Cobwebs covered in frost hung before them and around them as if suspended on invisible thread, and the thick grass was brittle with hard white frost which crackled beneath them as Daisy placed her feet. Jenny felt as if they had disappeared, enveloped in this soft, still, silent white moonscape. She gently halted Daisy, and they stood, surveying the scene all around them, breathing in the frozen air and listening to the silence. As they walked around the hilltop, the sun made a brief appearance and lit up the frosted grass. It looked as if someone had turned on ten thousand fairy lights, and the mist before them seemed to be full of gold and silver ribbons.

Jenny glanced at her watch and realised she had been out far longer than she had intended. She put her hand just underneath Daisy's exercise rug and could feel that Daisy was still lovely and warm. They headed downhill and made their way home very carefully, passing through layers of cloud as they descended. Gradually, the temperature rose a little, although they were more than halfway down before they were able to see the tops of the trees around the yard. By the time they reached the bottom of the hill, in spite of the hard frost, it felt much warmer than it had at the top. Jenny dismounted to lead Daisy into the yard and put her back into her stable. The hilltop had had a magical quality and, she thought, it was not something she might see again for a long time. She felt quite exhilarated by the experience and was glad she had made the effort to take Daisy out.

CHAPTER TWENTY-THREE

BAD NEWS

After making Daisy comfortable and putting away the tack, Jenny went to find Tina to return her exercise sheet. Tina was in the office talking to Wendy – she looked a little upset and both girls stopped talking and looked towards the door as Jenny entered. Tina turned and left the office without a word. Jenny could sense the atmosphere and was concerned.

"Is she OK?" she asked Wendy.

Wendy didn't reply, just rubbed her forehead with her fingers as if she had a headache, then she said, "Jenny, sit down please. I have some bad news, I'm afraid."

Jenny sat down anxiously, feeling her stomach turn over in apprehension. She waited. Wendy cleared her throat.

"Jenny," she said, "I am so sorry, so very sorry, but I have to give you a month's notice, with effect from Saturday, that your loan agreement for Daisy has to end."

Jenny felt a rush of heat run through her, she felt dizzy and unable to speak. She opened her mouth to say something, but no words came.

"Why?" she managed eventually, staring at Wendy in disbelief. "Why? Have I done something wrong?"

"No, no, my dear, you have done nothing wrong, far from it. I am so sorry."

"Will… will I still be able to ride her?" asked Jenny hesitantly.

"No, I'm afraid not," Wendy shook her head apologetically, "and there is absolutely nothing I can do."

"Why?" asked Jenny, feeling sick with shock. "Why?" She felt the tears start to roll and could do nothing to stop them.

"Daisy is being sold, my dear. I know how much she means to you. I have tried my hardest to prevent this from happening but without success. She is being sold and taken away."

Sold. Jenny's heart skipped a beat. *Sold.* She could hardly believe it. *Sold.* "But why?" she asked with a gulp. "Why are you selling her?"

"The gentleman who leases the yard to me, his daughter Sheila went to school with Felicity's mother and they are still great friends. Felicity and her family are moving to a bigger house with land – they want to keep horses and Felicity wants Daisy. I have told them that Daisy is not really a child's pony. I have pointed out that I have other ponies which are far more suitable, but Felicity has always adored Daisy and has cried herself to sleep for a week at the thought that she can't have her. So her mother is going to buy Daisy and take her with them."

Jenny was too shocked to know what to say. She stared glumly at the floor. It had never occurred to her that her loan arrangement might end. The month's notice on either side was, she thought, so that the client could give notice if they were moving, or could no longer afford to ride. She had met clients who had had their horses on loan for several years, and even the ones who ultimately bought them still kept them at the yard as it was so familiar to them. Sold. Daisy sold. She felt sick. She just had to get out of there, go home; she couldn't bear it if anyone came into the office now and saw her like this.

"I have to go," she mumbled and, without looking at Wendy, ran back to her car and drove home.

Jenny couldn't stop the tears falling throughout the drive home, and once indoors she threw herself onto her bed without taking her coat off and sobbed and sobbed. She had thrown her heart and soul into making progress with her riding and had dedicated herself entirely to riding Daisy as well as she could. She had looked after Daisy, cared for her more than was strictly required of her and had loved every minute of it. She had thought that the loan arrangement would continue indefinitely, as it had with the other regulars around the yard, and had hoped that she might have jumping lessons too. She knew Daisy would enjoy that, and maybe eventually they could enter a competition or two and come home with some ribbons and a framed photograph of them both. Daisy was the best thing to happen to Jenny in years. She adored her, thought of little else but Daisy and riding; her immersion in this new pleasure had been total. She had been truly happy these past few months, the happiest she had ever been. To think that all this would be taken away in a few weeks and that she would never ride Daisy ever again, was more than she could bear. The tears began to flow more profusely. She was suddenly interrupted by a loud knock on the door.

I can't answer it like this, she thought to herself, lifting her head sufficiently to look at her bedraggled appearance in the dressing table mirror. The knock came again, then another, louder and more urgent. The clang of the letterbox flap opening made her jump.

"Jenny!" Tina's voice. "Jenny! Open the door!"

Jenny scrambled off the bed and straightened her clothes, running both hands through her hair as she went to open the door.

"This is a surprise!" she managed to say when she opened it.

"Well, I hope you're going to ask me in?" said Tina, raising her eyebrows.

"Of course, of course, sorry, please, please do come in. Can, can I g-get you a coffee or something?" stammered Jenny, feeling a bit self-conscious and embarrassed.

"Coffee would be fine, thanks. I brought chocolate."

And with a flourish, Tina produced a box of chocolate cakes from her bag. Jenny smiled weakly.

"Thank you," she said appreciatively. "That was very kind of you. You shouldn't have."

"I came to see how you were feeling," said Tina.

"It was a terrible shock," said Jenny, feeling the tears beginning to well up again behind her eyes. "It never occurred to me that the loan arrangement could suddenly end."

"Me neither," said Tina, "it's never happened before. Loan arrangements are a perfect solution for everyone. The horse gets personal attention as well as riding school experience and being part of a herd; the client has perfect cover for sickness and holidays; the yard has a ready band of tried and tested regular horses whose track record they know; and if the client moves away or has to stop riding for some reason, the horse is quite safe and doesn't have the upheaval of being sold to a complete stranger."

They had walked towards the kitchen as they were talking and Jenny now motioned Tina to a chair. Tina sat down and opened the box of cakes while Jenny filled the kettle.

"That's what I believed," said Jenny. "It seems so unfair. Is there absolutely nothing I can do?"

"I'm afraid not," said Tina, shaking her head. "It's a terrible shame for Daisy actually as I don't think she will enjoy being in such a quiet environment. I think she will miss the variety of work and the bustle of the yard, and she isn't, as we all know, ideal to be a children's pony in the first place, although she has never bitten or kicked or anything horrible like that. She seems to have a very kind heart, but she is quirky and mischievous."

"Yes," said Jenny, nodding and remembering the almost vertical gallop when she rode with Carole and Barney. She took the coffee mugs, milk and a cafetière of coffee to the table and went back to the cupboard for a plate for the cakes.

"I don't think I can bear to ride her for four more weeks, Tina," she said, shaking her head. "I think I shall just cry all the time I am with her, especially now I know I'm doing something for the last time."

"Nonsense!" said Tina briskly. "Daisy is still your responsibility for another four weeks for a start, and you have to realise, Jenny, that life with horses is like this. We all remember the pain of losing our first – either we outgrew it and it was sold, or it was injured and retired, or it reached old age and died. You've had dogs?"

Jenny nodded. "Many times and, yes, I see what you are trying to say. Nothing lasts forever, that's the way of life. It's just that it's so sudden, so soon…" She trailed off, feeling the heat of the unshed tears which were queueing up and ready to flow again.

"Happy memories of your dogs, though?" enquired Tina. Jenny nodded again. "Well, then! And so you will have of Daisy. My goodness, just look at what you have achieved in just a few months! Your riding has progressed in leaps and bounds; you understand the mare better than anyone else I know; you ride her better than any other client has ever done; she has a better exercise programme than anything else on the yard; and she is clearly contented and very, very fit. Too fit, in my view, to be a child's pony, but there we are. The deal is done, and we have to move on and look to the future. There are other horses, plenty of them, which want a bit of personal attention. So – we put the disappointment behind us and we look to the future, right? Deal?"

"I suppose so, yes," said Jenny, trying to sound enthusiastic for Tina's sake.

"Good girl," said Tina. "Phew, for a minute there I thought you might not want to come to my wedding either."

Jenny smiled. She was starting to feel better already, thanks to Tina.

"Have you sent the invitations out yet?" she asked, thinking that perhaps it was a good time to change the subject.

"Tomorrow," replied Tina, reaching for another cake, and she began to update Jenny on all the arrangements. Jenny was grateful for her friend's visit and, when Tina left her much later after another pot of coffee and a round of sandwiches, Jenny felt considerably better, apart from a fleeting thought that soon Tina would go out of her life as well as Daisy.

She tried not to think about it anymore as she drifted off to sleep.

Chapter Twenty-Four

The Drag Hunt

The following morning dawned bright and clear, with a brisk cold breeze under a blue sky. Occasional fluffy white clouds temporarily blocked a valiant sun which made little difference to the temperature but was a cheerful sight. When Jenny awoke, her first thought was that it was a good day to ride, although Daisy would probably be quite lively as they had only walked on the previous two days. Once, she had been hacking and had met one of the villagers, who had said to her, "Nice day to ride, miss!"

She had replied that every day was a nice day to ride, you just had to be wearing the right clothes. With a jolt she suddenly remembered the events of the afternoon before, the conversation with Wendy, and Tina's visit. Her stomach lurched as she felt sadness sweep over her again. *Come on, girl*, she thought to herself, *you have one month left. Why not make the very best of every single moment?*

Her resolve strengthened, she got up immediately, showered very quickly, had a hurried breakfast and was standing outside Daisy's stable door within the hour.

"Right, young lady," she said as Daisy looked up and saw her, nickered her usual greeting and came over to the door for a pat, still chewing a mouth full of hay, "an early start for us today."

Jenny left her to finish breakfast and went off to the tack room to collect all their kit.

Tina walked past them pushing a wheelbarrow, as Jenny was mounting in the cobbled yard. "OK?" she enquired.

Jenny nodded. "Better, thank you," she replied. "I'm going to make the most of every single minute I have left."

"Good lass," said Tina, smiling as she moved off towards the barn to fill up her wheelbarrow with clean straw.

Daisy was keen to be off and had her head up and a spring in her step as they left the yard. Jenny had decided to ride through the village and take the path alongside the canal so that they could have a nice canter along the field edge. As she passed the cottage where she had seen Matthew and his mother, she nudged Daisy into a trot and kept her eyes on the garden, just in case the dog was loose and ran after them. The front door opened and Matthew ran out, closely followed by his mother.

"Good morning, miss!" the lady called.

"Good morning!" Jenny called back as she brought Daisy to a halt.

"Can our Matthew come and pat your 'orse, miss?" the lady asked.

"Yes, of course he can," replied Jenny with a smile as Matthew ran out of the gate and hurtled towards Daisy's back legs.

"Matthew! Matthew! Wait for me!" his mother shouted after him as she came down the little garden path and out onto the village street.

"He loves horses, he does, miss," she said to Jenny when she arrived at Daisy's shoulder. "He loves 'em. Wants to ride, he does, miss. I said when he's older. He watches all the 'orses what pass and he just loves 'em. You can't pat 'em all though, miss, some don't stop, see."

Jenny nodded. "Best to keep clear of the big horses perhaps; the ponies are more used to children."

"Birthday!" said Matthew. "Birthday!" as he thumped Daisy's leg with a chubby fist.

"Is it your birthday, Matthew?" asked Jenny.

"It's tomorrow, miss, 'e'll be three, 'e will."

"Three!" exclaimed Jenny. "That sounds very exciting, Matthew. Happy birthday for tomorrow."

"We're 'aving tea," said Matthew's mother. "We made a cake an' all. Why don't you come, miss?"

"I'd love to," said Jenny.

"And your 'orse, miss, gotta bring your 'orse; my dad'll love 'er."

"Oh, yes, thank you," said Jenny hesitantly, wondering how on earth she was supposed to take Daisy to a three-year-old's birthday tea party but not wanting to be rude and refuse.

"What time shall we come?" she asked.

"Three o'clock, miss, three o'clock will be grand, miss," said Matthew's mother, beaming.

"Well, we shall look forward to that, won't we, Daisy?" Jenny said as she leaned forward and patted Daisy's neck.

"Bye bye. Until tomorrow, then," Jenny said brightly. "Bye bye, Matthew!" and he waved to them both as she nudged Daisy into walk and continued on down the lane.

They had not gone very far before Daisy began to strut and prance and, although she showed no sign of taking off and Jenny was still able to hold her, it was an uncomfortable gait to ride and took all of Jenny's concentration and balance.

"What on earth has got into you, Daisy?" she asked her, and wondered whether the entire ride was going to be like this. *Perhaps, she thought, once they had had a canter Daisy would calm down a little.* The prancing and bouncing worsened and, as Jenny was wondering whether she should turn back towards the yard, she heard the sounds of a horn and dogs barking, blowing on the wind towards them.

Oh help! she thought. *It's a drag hunt.* Jenny knew there was a local group which occasionally rode to hounds and they followed a scent trail. One or two of the girls at the yard had ridden with the group and said that galloping around in a group was enormous fun, made more exciting by not knowing at any moment which way the trail would twist or turn. Daisy must have been able to hear them from a long way off, hence the prancing and cavorting.

Jenny was not sure what to do. Daisy by now was snorting and tossing her head wildly as well as prancing up and down, and she was getting stronger by the minute.

I daren't canter her like this, Jenny thought to herself, trying hard to sit to the very uncomfortable bouncy motion and keep her hands as low as possible.

"Check your position." She could hear Tina's voice in her head. *"Heels down, take a deep breath."* Jenny thought they would do best to stick to the roads as she had no idea whereabouts the hunt was, or which direction they were heading in, and goodness knows what would happen if they bumped into the hunt and ended up galloping off with them! It did not bear thinking about.

Daisy was beginning to whip herself up into a frenzy, the snorting and head tossing became almost impossible to manage, and although they were moving forwards it was in a very chaotic fashion rather than any sort of straight line. Foam and lather began to develop upon Daisy's neck and shoulders, and Jenny could feel the heat rising from her. She was praying that Daisy did not make any attempt to canter down the tarmac road, as she would be likely to slip on her metal shoes and potentially hurt them both. She managed to turn Daisy to the left along a narrow track between trees, which in turn soon led onto a lane where there was a crossroads and they could turn right to head back towards the yard.

However, the horn sounded again and the hunt seemed even nearer. Foam was flying off Daisy's neck onto Jenny's arms and she was worn out with the concentration of trying to maintain her balance and hold the reins amidst Daisy's frantic head tossing! As they approached the crossroads a red car came into view, and the driver, upon seeing her difficulty, stopped to wait for her to pass. Normally, Jenny was very strict about road drill, but today Daisy simply wasn't listening to anything but the feverish frenzy in her head.

"Daisy!" Jenny spoke loudly and sharply, hoping it might get her attention. "Halt!" Exasperated, Jenny thought to herself, *I will* not *have the traffic stop for us because she won't behave.*

"Daisy!" she said more sternly now. "Stand still!"

Whether Daisy did indeed hear her, or whether the combination of her stern voice and sitting very tall in her saddle and shortening her rein even more made the difference, or whether perhaps Daisy was indeed beginning to tire from her overexertions, Jenny knew not, but she just managed to halt her sufficiently well for just a few seconds to be able to nod, smile and wave the car on. Once the road was clear she gave just a tiny bit with her reins and together they bounced like an erratic rubber ball to the other side of the road.

They were not far from the yard now, and as they approached the gate Daisy began to calm a little. By the time they walked onto the yard the bouncing had become more of a high-stepping prance. Billie was on the seat in the sunshine with her lunchbox as they went past the office.

"Great Scott!" she exclaimed. "Whatever happened to you? Daisy looks as if she's just run the 3.30 at Cheltenham!"

"We bumped into the drag hunt," said Jenny. "Madam was beside herself with excitement. I had a terrible job getting us both back here safely."

"Good heavens. Well done you!" said Billie. "You need to cool her off and get a Thermatex on her straight away, Jenny; it's a cold day and we don't want her to catch a chill. The kettle's just boiled; take her round to the yard and I'll bring you some warm water."

Billie stood up immediately to go back into the office, and by the time Jenny had tied Daisy up Billie had arrived with a bucket of warm water, a sponge, a sweat scraper and a special type of rug to help Daisy to dry off and cool down.

"You will have to pop her back in her stable for an hour before she's turned out, Jenny. Please skip it out when you have finished, it's all ready for bedtime."

"Will do," said Jenny. "Thank you for your help, Billie."

"By the way," said Billie as she turned to go, "I was sorry to hear the news. You two are an item. I have always thought you were absolutely perfect for one another. She has taught you a great deal and I believe she has benefitted from knowing you too. She seems very happy indeed, but I'm sure we will find something else for you that you can enjoy just as much, Jenny."

"I hope so," Jenny replied, nodding. She turned away and looked down as she did so, hoping that Billie would not see that her eyes had filled with tears. She blinked hard to try to regain her composure as she led Daisy round to her stable.

Daisy made a beeline for her pile of hay as soon as Jenny unclipped her head collar.

"Worked up an appetite, have we?!" Jenny said to her. "You and me both, Daisy! I'm off to the office for a bar of chocolate. I'll be back soon."

As Jenny left the stable and slid the big bolt over the door, Daisy rushed to the door to put her head out and watch Jenny go. Having satisfied herself that she was not missing anything important, she went back to her hay straight away. By the time Jenny returned some thirty minutes later, Daisy was in the middle of her stable with her head hanging down, dozing. Jenny's arrival woke her up and she nickered softly.

"I think we'll get you ready to go out for a while," Jenny said to her. "Ah, I can see we have to skip you out. I'll get the bucket."

Jenny left the stable to reach for a metal bucket which stood outside the stable door. Each stable had one – it was used for skipping out the boxes last thing at night so that both horses and stables were that much cleaner in the morning. Having picked up the pile of droppings and deposited it into the bucket, Jenny was just about to turn to leave and take it out to the muck heap when Daisy walked towards the door, turned in a full circle until she was standing in the centre of the stable, and spread her legs.

"If you are going to pee, pee in this!" said Jenny, quickly thrusting the bucket underneath Daisy's back end.

Daisy obliged instantly and Jenny grinned as she removed the bucket.

"Clever girl!" she said with amusement as she gave Daisy's neck a good rub. "Now your nice clean stable will be both clean *and* dry for tonight."

A few moments later, after Jenny had rugged Daisy up, she took her down to the paddock. As she let her loose, she was surprised to see that, instead of strolling forwards a few paces and dropping her head to graze as she usually did, this time Daisy set off at a fast canter like a bullet out of a gun and bucked and bucked and bucked. By the time she had covered the length of the paddock, every other horse had joined in and they all made two laps around the outside of the field before collectively blowing down their noses and settling down again to graze.

Mmmm... thought Jenny, *I am so glad I wasn't on board this time. Get it out of your system, Daisy. Tomorrow we canter...*

CHAPTER TWENTY-FIVE
HERDING SHEEP

The following morning Jenny arrived at Daisy's stable before she had finished her morning hay. This routine of riding earlier and having more time in the paddock afterwards was probably better for Daisy during winter, Wendy had said, and she had suggested that if Jenny wanted to clean tack and potter about the yard for a few hours, she could bring Daisy in when the other horses came in for tea. Jenny had not yet had the opportunity to help with bringing in and putting Daisy to bed, and loved the idea of having this additional experience, even if only for a month.

Jenny had decided that if they were going to go to a tea party – although how that was to happen she so far had not a clue – then Daisy needed to have the wind taken out of her sails in advance. A good canter or two across the hills seemed to be the order of the day, and Jenny was a little nervous at the prospect having seen Daisy's bucking demonstration in the paddock on the previous afternoon! She had mentioned it to Tina, who had reassured her that letting off steam was confined to high jinks in the paddock and Daisy was not the sort of horse to behave like that with a rider on board.

However, in spite of the reassurance, Jenny made sure that Tina knew her proposed route for the morning exactly and what time she would expect to be back. Tina had suggested that Jenny should send a text when they were safely on their way home and she had said she would.

By now, there were very few routes that Jenny could not deal with on her own, as she had made a great deal of progress with refining the art of opening and closing gates. Occasionally, she was most amused when she directed Daisy to go to, for example, the left side of the gate when it looked to Jenny as if the catch was situated on that side, only to have Daisy ignore her instruction and head for the right side instead, where, sure enough, the catch actually turned out to be. The good news was that Jenny had never yet had to dismount for a gate and hoped that she would never have to. She was not sure whether Daisy would be patient enough to wait for her, or whether she would instead wander off to graze and refuse to be caught. The grass was extremely lush up on the hill and Jenny didn't want to take the chance.

The hills were covered in sheep, which made winter hacks all the more interesting and challenging. The sheep were incredibly indecisive and appeared to deliberate over whether to cross Daisy's path or not, and invariably, once they had decided not to, they would watch Daisy's approach intently and then change their minds at the last minute and catapult themselves in front of her at top speed. The best canters were unfortunately strewn with sheep and, in the interests of safety, Jenny had devised a rule that no matter how keen they may be, they would slow their canter to a walk when close to sheep and, once clear, would immediately canter again. To her credit, Daisy seemed to understand this new rule perfectly and had so far not offered any resistance to Jenny's plan.

Today, they met another obstacle on their way to the top of the hill. Some sheep had escaped the field and were all over the track! The gate was swinging open and Jenny was concerned that the sheep which were loose might wander off or come to some harm and that those still in the field might join the escapees. She felt duty bound to try and do something to put them back in the field, so tried to get Daisy to circle them to drive them back towards the gate.

Whether Daisy had done this sort of thing before, or whether this was an entirely new game for her, Jenny did not know, but Daisy seemed a natural at shepherding, dropping her head and neck really low and tossing her head towards the sheep. Jenny giggled as she thought that, to the sheep, Daisy must look like a very large goose! It took a while, as there was always one loose sheep which decided to bolt once all the others were back inside, but eventually they were all safely back. Jenny discovered that the gate was actually broken and she had to dismount to see if she could find a way to secure it. She held on tightly to the end of Daisy's reins while she tried to secure the gate with the other hand. Daisy, meanwhile, hovered around the gate like a four-legged goalie, daring any reckless sheep to cross her path. When they had finished, Jenny hopped back on quickly before making a big fuss of Daisy.

"What a star you are!" she said enthusiastically. "Good girl, Daisy! Come on, let's go and have a really good canter now as a treat."

They made their way up to the very large field which they had visited only a few days before when it resembled a moonscape, and Jenny was surprised that Daisy did not seem desperate to take off and have a good romp. Instead, she was incredibly polite and waited for every signal as they transitioned to trot and then canter. Jenny was so pleased with Daisy's conduct, in comparison to the previous morning when they were so near the hunt, that she leaned forward whilst in motion and gave Daisy a big pat on her neck.

"Gosh, I shall miss you, girlie," she said, feeling suddenly overcome with emotion again. "I do hope they learn to love you as much as I do." She felt the tears well up behind her eyes, and as she cantered along, tears streaming down her face, she pressed her leg against Daisy's side to encourage her to open up and go faster, fast enough to leave her tears behind. As the two of them sped across the soft turf in an elegant rhythm, Jenny closed her eyes and felt herself melt into Daisy's back. The two of them were one, united both in movement and in spirit, flying over the thick soft grass as free as the air around them, one, two, three, one, two, three, one, two, three…

CHAPTER TWENTY-SIX
THE TEA PARTY

J enny had thought long and hard about the etiquette of taking Daisy to a tea party and what she should wear, and had decided upon the red travel rug, a bridle with the reins lashed under the throat and a very light, matching red head collar underneath. Hopefully, control was there if needed, but Jenny would have her hands relatively free as she only had to hold onto a lead rope. Thankfully no rain was forecast and she decided to wear her navy jodhpurs, a thick cream sweater with a scarf around the neck to dress it up a little bit and a navy quilted gilet. She had stopped at the newsagents the day before to buy a small toy for

Matthew from the 'pocket-money toys' display. The toy was a set of a drum with drumsticks and a whistle; Jenny imagined that Matthew might enjoy banging a drum and blowing a whistle, and she hoped he did not already have them.

Daisy walked very nicely in hand from the yard to the cottage and they arrived promptly at 3 p.m. There were balloons outside the front door and some more attached to the gate by string. Daisy wasn't sure whether the balloons were friend or foe, and Jenny had to encourage her to get close and have a little look at them. As they were doing this Matthew's mother appeared at the door.

"Round this way, miss, round this way!" she called cheerily with a wave of her hand towards the green wooden double gate which led onto the lane from the end of the garden. She hurried towards it, wiping her hands on her apron as she did so, and opened it for them to pass through.

Jenny followed her and with Daisy in hand, they walked up the short drive towards a large wooden lean-to which had been erected just outside the back door. There was a log store to one side of the lean-to, and a small coop of chickens in an old wire run scratched about in the dirt next to an immaculate vegetable plot.

Jenny hoped that the dog was locked in somewhere and would not put in an appearance and was then horrified when it suddenly rushed out of the back door and headed straight for Daisy's feet, barking noisily. It was a youngish thin sheepdog, which seemed to be in several places at once and did not keep still for a minute.

It yapped at Daisy and lowered itself to the ground and moved backwards.

"Stop it, Pups! Stop it! Quiet now!" Matthew's mother yelled at it. The dog took no notice and ran towards Daisy again. To Jenny's relief she did not seem to mind one bit and lowered her head as if to peer at the animal more closely. This sent Pups into a panic, and it scuttled backwards, yelping, before turning and rushing back into the house.

"Gramps! Gramps!" shouted Matthew's mother, and an elderly man appeared at the back door. In spite of wearing leather slippers he was dressed for the cold with a thick sweater and waistcoat, a flat cap and woollen scarf.

"Hello, missy," he said, stretching out his hand to Jenny and smiling broadly. "And who's the lovely lady?" motioning to Daisy as he shuffled forwards along the path.

"What a beauty, what a beauty!" he said with feeling as he reached Daisy and stroked the length of her nose with the back of one wrinkled brown hand. "What a beauty!"

Matthew shot out of the back door at that moment, accompanied by the dog and three other little boys of about the same age. He appeared to be holding something, and the others chased him around the garden before he evaded them and shot back indoors again, with the barking dog, which was jumping up to snatch at whatever was in his hand. Matthew's mother appeared at the door to ask if they both wanted tea and that gave Jenny an opportunity to hand her the little present for Matthew.

"Oh that's kind of you, miss. You shouldn't 'ave, thank you," she said. "I've put the littl'uns in the kitchen in case their noise frightens the 'orse."

"She don't mind, do you, my lovely?" said the old man as he produced two tall stools from the back of the lean-to and offered one to Jenny.

Daisy followed his every movement and turned her head to listen when he spoke, as captivated by him as he was by her. He explained to Jenny that he had been a farrier for fifty-five years. He clearly adored all horses and was delighted that both his sons had followed the same profession. Matthew's father had a very good job at a big race yard in the next county and lived on site with the other farriers and grooms, but he came home for four days once every two weeks. To Jenny's absolute delight, Daisy seemed entirely at home spending time with this little family, standing outside their back door sharing tea and cake from a small picnic table. She thrilled them all by lapping weak black tea from one of the dog's bowls and, after sharing a piece of cake with Jenny, she raised her head high and flared her lips, which made them all laugh.

Matthew's mother brought the children out to see a repeat performance of Daisy drinking the tea, and they squealed with delight, before rushing back indoors again excitedly to fetch the drum, so that Matthew could proudly demonstrate his skill as a drummer. One of the other little boys accompanied him on the whistle and, as the adults raised their voices to be heard above the din, the dog, oblivious to the noise, re-appeared and settled happily at Gramps' feet. Like Daisy, he watched the old man intently. When it began to get dark Matthew's mum lit some candles which were in jam-jars hanging from the shed roof on string. Jenny was almost sorry when the time came to go, and Matthew was most amused to know that they had to go as it was nearly Daisy's bedtime. He kept asking his mother how old Daisy was because he did not have to be in bed for another two hours. Eventually, having said thank you and goodbye several times and promising to return again soon, they made their way back towards the yard while Matthew and his family waved them off.

Chapter Twenty-Seven

Night-Time in the Stable

Jenny loved the atmosphere of the yard in the early evening, after all the horses had been brought in for the night. Some stood with their heads over their stable doors, their breath steamy in the cold night air, watching the yard girls moving in and out of the stables, finishing the last chores of the day. Water buckets had to be checked and replenished, and the stables skipped out so that they were clean before their occupants' long night in, then the rugs which had been hanging over stable doors were carried off to the rug room to dry. Jenny particularly loved the cosy feel of Daisy's stable and stood inside the door for a while, watching Daisy sort through her sweet-smelling pile of fluffy hay. It had only taken her five minutes to enthusiastically scoff the contents of the feed bowl and, after chasing the last morsels around and around the bowl with her tongue, she had eventually lost interest, tipped the bowl upside down and trodden on it.

She rushed to the stable door and looked out eagerly as if she had heard something unusual.

"What is it, Daisy?" asked Jenny as Daisy tossed her head towards the end of the yard before quickly bringing it back into the stable, walking around in a tight circle and then rushing back to the door again to put her head out a second time. She nickered as she did so and Jenny moved over to the door to see what Daisy was looking at.

"Sorry, Daisy," she said, "I don't understand, poppet. What did you hear?"

While Jenny was speaking, she opened the door and slipped out of it, holding it shut with one hand while she reached for the metal bucket to skip Daisy out. As she stepped back into the stable, closing the door behind her, Daisy nickered again and tossed her head at the bucket.

"It isn't anything to eat, Daisy. I..." She broke off, laughing as she realised what it was that Daisy wanted. Daisy circled again, stopped and began to spread her legs, and Jenny quickly thrust the metal bucket underneath her and waited while she peed into it.

"You didn't hear anything, did you? You wanted me to get the bucket so you could pee into it." Jenny giggled again, whisking the bucket away the minute Daisy had finished, lest she move her back legs inwards, kick the bucket and knock it over.

"You are a very clever girl, Daisy May," she said as she ruffled Daisy's mane affectionately.

"I will go and empty this and then I must go home."

Is it exasperating to be a horse and not be able to make yourself understood when you want something? Jenny wondered, and just for a moment she felt a little sad that both the bond and the mutual understanding which had developed, and was continuing to develop, between herself and Daisy seemed to be growing stronger by the day and yet she knew that very soon it would all come to an abrupt end. Would Felicity's family enjoy, as she did, Daisy's ability to make herself understood and to reason? Jenny remembered the incident at the water trough a few months earlier, when Daisy had solved a problem which was affecting all the other horses; the way she stepped in and took charge when the hack had to go past the road menders; the cavalry charge on the heathland during the coast ride where she had endeavoured to turn the ponies back towards the waiting riders. She thought about Daisy's actions when they had fallen into the waterlogged muddy rut and Daisy had saved the day and got them safely back onto firm ground, and her insistence that they had turned in the wrong direction when Jenny made a mistake.

Know when to insist and when to respect their instinct – the phrase re-played in her head. Jenny could see that it would be most reckless to suggest to anyone learning to ride that they let the horse take charge and do what it wanted to do, but this wasn't what was happening between her and Daisy. This was a real and true partnership, neither of them was solely 'in charge' of their safety, the responsibility was shared and, yes, she as the rider of course had the ultimate control should she need it. She had not forgotten the difficulty she had had trying to control Daisy with the drag hunt so near, nor the almost vertical gallop when they were out with Carole, but as a percentage of all the time they had spent together Daisy's misbehaviour was minimal.

CHAPTER TWENTY-EIGHT

THE CHRISTMAS GYMKHANA

The winter days seemed to be speeding by at twice their usual pace, and hacking was made more difficult because of the weather. It was either very wet and windy or extremely cold and icy, and once or twice Jenny had to make use of the indoor school instead of leaving the yard. When she rode, her feet and hands froze, no matter what she wore, and for two consecutive days it was too icy even to take the horses out of their stables at all, and the girls had to muck out half a stable at a time while its occupant stood in the other half with a hay net. Christmas at the yard was celebrated with a gymkhana which everyone said was always enormous fun.

This year, to keep competitors and spectators alike warm and dry, the indoor school had been set up as a jumping arena, with straw bales piled in tiers at one end to make rows of seating like a theatre. The outdoor schools were to be used for warm-ups and practice, and canvas sheeting had been rigged up, to make a waterproof corridor for riders moving from the warm-up arena to the indoor school for the competition and back again. Jenny went to watch and to help with mid-morning refreshments, but more especially to watch Daisy take part in the jumping and some of the games against the clock during the afternoon. Daisy often seemed to be disregarding the signals of her young rider completely, and Jenny noticed several times that Daisy pre-empted the bell and leapt into action the moment it sounded, whether or not the rider was either ready or had asked her to. Tina rode her in the adult section and won her class, with Carole coming second on Barney. Tina also rode a pretty grey mare called Tallow which was new to the yard and had been ridden side-saddle as well as the more traditional way; it could be jumped side-saddle as well. Jenny thought side-saddle looked extremely precarious and couldn't imagine how you could jump side-saddle but meant to try it one day.

Wendy handed out the prizes and, when she presented Tina with hers, she made a little speech thanking her for all her loyalty and hard work and saying how much she would be missed. There had been a collection for a wedding present for Tina and her husband-to-be, and Wendy presented her with a fantastic coffee-making machine on behalf of them all. Jenny thought the gift most appropriate, knowing Tina's love of coffee! The day ended with a big bonfire and a barbecue manned by some of the husbands and partners of the staff, and Jenny thoroughly enjoyed mingling with some of the other clients, sipping mulled wine in the firelight, with the tang of barbecue smoke and sausages lingering in the air around them. The conversation revolved exclusively around horses, and Jenny found herself longing to have a horse of her own to love and care for. She felt a lump in her throat at the thought that even if she could ever afford it, which was highly unlikely, it could never be Daisy, with her quirky ways, her intelligence, her problem-solving abilities and her enthusiasm for life. Jenny felt tears filling her eyes, and she was just about to turn and head for the ladies to compose herself when Tina appeared at her side.

"Are you having a good time?" she asked. Her face was flushed from standing too near the fire and Jenny thought how radiantly happy she looked.

"Fantastic! Great party. Congratulations, by the way! I thought the jumping was wonderful."

"She is such a good mare for jumping; she makes it so easy," said Tina, waving a hand as if to brush off the praise. "What did you think of Tallow?"

"She looked very sweet. Is she easy to ride?" asked Jenny.

"Textbook," replied Tina. "I wondered if she might be a good replacement for Daisy? The sooner you find something that suits you the better, you know, especially if you want another loan arrangement."

Jenny nodded. "Yes, I know, it's just that I... Maybe it's too soon. I – I hadn't..." Her voice trailed off as she struggled to control the flow of the tears which streamed down her face.

"Oh, lass," said Tina kindly, putting her arms around her, "I do so wish things were different for you. But, you know, they are all special in one way or another. You may never find another bright and quirky little mischief like Daisy, but different doesn't mean worse, you know, it just means different. Have you ever thought of buying your own?"

"Out of the question," said Jenny firmly, shaking her head. "I could never afford it, and anyway I still have so much to learn, it probably wouldn't be fair to the horse."

Tina nodded her understanding. "You will keep in touch, won't you?" she said, deftly changing the subject. "I have had some cards printed. I'll give them out next week so that everyone has my contact details. I would love you to come and stay the minute we are settled. You will come, won't you? I reckon I shall be able to open the yard after about six weeks; we have everything in place and I even have the promise of one or two really nice horses which need a good home. I may offer weekend workshops eventually, and people can bring their horses for an overnight stay."

"Of course I will come. I would love to. I'm dying to see the farm. It all sounds amazing and I hope it will be a fantastic success," said Jenny enthusiastically, her composure regained.

The party eventually ended and, as cars started to drive away, with their occupants calling goodnight to one another through open windows, Jenny thought she would just go round to the cobbled yard and say goodnight to Daisy. There was a full moon, no breeze and the yard seemed awfully quiet and very dark indeed where there were no security lights. Jenny wondered if she might be doing the wrong thing and, for an instant, thought some sort of intruder alarm might be set off by her presence, but fortunately there was none. At her approach, Daisy popped her head over the door and nickered softly.

"Did you hear me or smell me, Daisy?" she asked, thinking that it was probably both. "I have come to say goodnight," she said, as she put both arms around Daisy's neck and stroked the warm, soft, slightly moist skin underneath Daisy's mane.

"Do you know, Daisy, just in case I never get another chance to tell you, you have been the most amazing friend and I shall never ever forget you." She stroked Daisy's nose then kissed the spot. Daisy didn't move, as Jenny closed her eyes and stood there for a moment, trying to record in her memory the feel and the smell of her beloved friend so that she could keep it with her always. They stood there for some time, neither of them moving, silent beneath the moonlight, in the still night air.

CHAPTER TWENTY-NINE
FAREWELL, DAISY

The last day of Jenny's loan arrangement was circled in black on her calendar, and Jenny had given some thought as to what they would most enjoy together over the last few days. A really good canter was essential, she thought, and a walk through the village another must, this time hopefully without the drag hunt. Fortunately the weather had settled and the outlook for the rest of the week was dry but cold, although without frost. With three days to go, she decided to revisit the very first place where she had learned to canter, The Cutting. Jenny made sure they set off nice and early and, as they left the yard, she recalled the first time ever she had gone out with Tina, how frightened she had been that Daisy might steal an opportunity to take off with her. Yet all that had been on Daisy's mind had been finding a big enough bush so that she could pee out of the wind without splashing her legs! Jenny grinned to herself at the memory. *How funny*, she thought. *What a long way I have come in less than a year.*

She took the opportunity to sing a marching song in time with Daisy's walk as they made their way along the track and turned towards The Cutting and the little wooden gate. The canter seemed remarkably short, in comparison to how it had felt just a few months ago, and she decided to make her way to The Little Gallop where Daisy had waited for her when she fell off. The wind was stronger up there and Daisy fidgeted a little as they closed the gate, eager to turn and take advantage of the soft flat green open space before them. Jenny barely had the time to ask for the transition before Daisy was off and into a fast canter. Jenny loosened the rein so that her friend could have her head, and they sped up the field in a beautifully smooth rhythm before pulling up quite late near the fence. *Gosh, that was good*, thought Jenny. *One of the smoothest, fastest canters we have ever had I should think.* She turned Daisy, to head back to the exit gate, and then the thought struck her – *We will not be able to do this together next week.*

"Hey, Daisy," she said, "that was amazing. Shall we do it again?"

To her amusement Daisy nodded her head up and down enthusiastically. "Come on, then, let's have an action replay!" said Jenny.

They made their way back to the start of the canter before taking off a second time, and once they reached the fence at the end Jenny could feel that Daisy was satisfied.

"Where would you like to go now, Daisy?" she asked, suddenly wondering: if Daisy knew this was one of their last rides, where would she like to go? What would she like to do? Only one way to find out, thought Jenny to herself, and when they reached the track she halted Daisy with the words, "Over to you, Daisy," then she dropped the rein to the buckle and gave Daisy a pat. She then sat completely still without giving any signal at all.

Jenny wondered whether Daisy would just stand there and wait for her signal, but instead she seemed to understand what was being asked and was perfectly happy to assume responsibility for deciding the route. She chose one of the tracks around the base of the hill, which ultimately took them back to the village and up the village street. Jenny felt almost elated that she had had such a good morning and was pleased that she had allowed Daisy the freedom to make the choice about their route home. It was still only late morning and Jenny still had many hours to enjoy at the yard, turning Daisy out and later bringing her in and putting her to bed.

When they reached Daisy's stable, there was a note pinned to it in Wendy's handwriting, asking Jenny to pop into the office. Jenny's heart skipped a beat and her mouth went dry. *What for?* she wondered. *Had Felicity had second thoughts? Had her mother realised that looking after horses full-time was too much for the family? Was Daisy staying at the yard, after all? There were only two days to go... gosh, what if it was all going to be OK? Oh please, please, please... let it be OK...* With trembling fingers she quickly untacked Daisy and made sure there was enough hay and water before making her way to the office. Wendy was there, talking to Felicity's mother, a pot of coffee and a half eaten plate of biscuits between them.

"Hello, Jenny!" said Wendy brightly when Jenny entered. "Thank you for coming in. Have you met Mrs Nugent?"

Jenny smiled and moved forward to shake hands with Felicity's mother.

"I have a favour to ask you, Jenny. We'd like you to help us out if you can," Wendy went on.

Jenny smiled but said nothing; in the back of her mind was a little voice whispering, Please, please, please... I'll help you out by keeping her on loan, no problem at all, please, please just ask...

"Mrs Nugent has some difficulties with the transport to take Daisy away at the weekend," Wendy continued, "and she wondered if it was possible to take her today instead? I said it would depend upon you as, strictly speaking, as you know, she is yours until the end of the week."

"I would be so grateful, my dear," Mrs Nugent interrupted, smiling at Jenny. "It has been so difficult to get transport arranged for the weekend when everyone is so terribly busy. It would be wonderful if she could come to us this afternoon – so much more convenient. We would, of course, be more than happy to compensate you for any loss."

Jenny was dumbstruck. She opened her mouth to speak but no words came, and she stood there foolishly staring at Mrs Nugent as if she had two heads. *Today*, she thought to herself, *today. That's it! It's over!*

"I... I..." she stammered.

"Will that be all right, Jenny?" Wendy interrupted her, nodding and smiling her encouragement as if willing her to agree.

"I... yes... ummm... of course, I..." Jenny trailed off lamely, not knowing quite what else to say.

She wanted to scream, shout. She could feel a build of emotion inside herself, like steam in a kettle, coursing through her veins – a mixture of shock at the sudden change to her plans and anger that this woman could just steal her last few days and think that all she had to do in exchange was give her some money! Suddenly she came to her senses.

"What time?" she asked briskly, looking from Wendy to Mrs Nugent and back again. Mrs Nugent looked at her watch.

"Shall we say 2:30 p.m., dear?" She looked at Wendy with a raised eyebrow.

"Fine by me," said Wendy. "All the paperwork is in place; I presume you have arranged insurance?"

Mrs Nugent nodded. "Everything is ready. Felicity is *so* excited!" she said, beaming. Wendy smiled.

"Is that all?" asked Jenny, thinking that if she didn't get out of the office immediately she would either scream or hit someone, preferably Mrs Nugent.

"Yes, Jenny, thank you," said Wendy, smiling at her, but Jenny was already half out of the door.

Jenny looked at her watch: 12:15 p.m. She felt completely at a loss as to know what to do next, and almost instinctively headed for Daisy's stable. The saddle and bridle were still outside ready to be put away, so she took them immediately back to the tack room, making a mental note to clean them later rather than waste any time.

Later on. Afterwards. When she's gone. I have *to keep busy*, she thought to herself.

She decided to give Daisy a thorough grooming so that at least she would be spotless when she left the yard. She had already cleaned her feet after their hack and before putting her back in her stable, but she spent a relaxing hour brushing Daisy's coat and brushing and combing her mane and tail until they gleamed like silk.

"You are the prettiest girl on the yard, you know, Daisy," she said, and felt a pang of sadness as Daisy turned to look at her and nodded her head, chewing on her hay thoughtfully, rather as someone might who had something to say and was deciding quite how to phrase it.

"No need to reply, Daisy," Jenny said to her with a grin as she patted her rump.

Jenny suddenly realised that she had no photos of Daisy except two which had been taken on the charity ride to the coast and, since Daisy was as beautifully groomed as she had ever been, Jenny went to get her mobile phone from the car to take some pictures. She was just closing the driver's door when she saw Mrs Nugent drive out of the yard.

Wendy was outside Daisy's stable when she returned, talking to one of the grooms.

"I'm really sorry about this, Jenny," said Wendy sincerely as she approached. "All of it, for what it's worth. We were just talking about what to dress Daisy in for her journey. I suppose the question is, do you want to be here when she goes? Would you like to put her travel clothes on a bit later? Or would you rather leave now?"

Jenny thought for a moment before replying.

"I think I would like to dress her, yes. I don't want to leave right this minute, but I don't think I could bear to watch her go."

"Exactly what I thought you would say," said Wendy. "OK, Sarah will bring the travel rug, tail wrap and boots round to your stable. Daisy will need to be dressed and ready to load at 2:15 p.m. She looks gorgeous, by the way, I can see there is no need to ask you to groom her first." She turned to go.

"And Jenny, please do pop over and see me tomorrow. Let's see what else we can do for you. Will you?"

Jenny nodded, but privately she was wondering whether she could bear to set foot on the yard for many weeks.

Once Wendy had gone, Jenny took a few photos of Daisy in her stable and, sadly, was quite disappointed with them. For one thing it was a little dark, and of course Daisy didn't understand how to pose for a photo, so most of them were of Daisy with her head down eating hay! Jenny kicked herself for not thinking about taking photos before this. In no time at all Sarah returned, and Jenny carefully dressed Daisy ready for her journey, talking to her all the while. At 2:15 p.m. she gave the mare a final hug, said goodbye, ruffled her mane for the last time, went back to her car and drove home. She felt numb, too numb even to cry.

CHAPTER THIRTY

EMPTINESS

Jenny did not slept terribly well; she kept wondering where Daisy was, was she OK? Did she understand that this change in her life was permanent? Were Felicity and her family being kind to her? She hoped they were and, indeed, had no reason to believe that Daisy would be anything other than loved and cared for to the utmost degree. Jenny eventually fell asleep and dreamed about the almost vertical gallop. In Jenny's dream they had galloped through the earth and arrived at a place which looked remarkably like The Little Gallop of their last canter together, except that it was seemingly endless.

The following morning, the telephone rang as Jenny was having breakfast.

"Hello?" Jenny answered.

"It's Wendy. How are you this morning, Jenny?"

"Fine, thank you," said Jenny, crossing her fingers behind her back as she said it.

"Are you free this morning?" Wendy went on. "Coffee at 11 a.m. if it suits you?"

Jenny hesitated. She really didn't feel able to go up to the yard so soon, and even the idea of riding, which would have thrilled her a year earlier, seemed to have lost its appeal overnight.

Ignoring her silence Wendy continued, "I really would appreciate a chat, Jenny. If it's no trouble?"

Jenny suddenly felt guilty. Wendy had always been immensely kind to her and it was not her fault that Daisy had had to be sold to the Nugent family, and she had apologised about it several times already. The least Jenny could do was have coffee with her.

"Of course, I would love to. 11 a.m. will be absolutely fine, Wendy."

"Oh good!" Jenny could hear the relief in Wendy's voice. "Eleven o'clock, then. I will look forward to it."

There were a lot of cars in the yard when Jenny arrived. Wendy told her later that there was a training event being held for students who were studying equine physiotherapy. Wendy already had the best coffee pot and a plate of luxurious chocolate biscuits on the table when Jenny arrived at the office.

"Ah, there you are," said Wendy with a smile. "Come and sit down, Jenny."

Jenny made herself comfortable and sipped her coffee while Wendy chatted generally about the training event and asked Jenny what she had thought of the gymkhana. Eventually, she said, "Now then, Jenny, I hope you want to continue with your riding. You have learned so much these past few months, it would be a shame to let it lapse. Carole tells me her mother is poorly and she needs to spend more time in the week looking after her, so she won't have as much opportunity to exercise Barney. We wondered if you would be able to help her out. He is always popular in the riding school of course, but Carole particularly liked the way you cared for Daisy and, as she hasn't had too much time to spare in recent weeks, she thought Barney might also enjoy a bit of TLC. What do you think?"

Jenny thought it over for a moment. She liked Carole and thought Barney was a nice-natured gelding, although perhaps a bit quiet. She had ridden him in school when she first started and had been glad of his calmness. She wasn't particularly keen on the idea but did not like to refuse; Carole was worried about her mother and had specifically asked for Jenny's help.

"I would be pleased to help, yes," she managed eventually, hoping that her lack of enthusiasm was not obvious.

"Good!" said Wendy brightly. "When would you like to come? We can have him ready for you the first time. What about Saturday? One of the girls can come out with you if you like; they all know him quite well."

Jenny could not think of anything to say which might sound like a genuine reason to delay, and she wished that Tina had not already left or they might have been able to ride together one last time. She nodded her agreement and Wendy reached for the appointments book to make a note for 11 a.m. on Saturday.

Jenny drove home shortly afterwards, not sure quite what to do with her day now that she had spare time on her hands. The weather was not particularly inspiring – thick grey clouds which showed no sign of moving hung heavily from the sky, and there was very little breeze; the atmosphere was damp and gloomy and the light was poor. *Even the weather feels miserable*, Jenny thought to herself, and she decided to stop at the supermarket on the way home to buy herself a pizza, a bottle of wine and a carton of her favourite ice cream. Once home, she drew the curtains and spent the rest of the day in her cosy sitting room, watching old films she had not seen for a while. She ate her evening meal much earlier than usual, was in bed by 9 p.m. and fast asleep shortly afterwards. The following day she busied herself with sorting out cupboards and drawers and taking unwanted items to the charity shop. She worked quite hard and, again, found that sleep came easily.

On Saturday morning Karen was on the list to accompany her, and Jenny arrived at Barney's stable just as he was being brought around to the mounting block. Karen was riding Spice, whom Jenny had not seen since the coast ride, apart from watching him jump in the gymkhana. Karen seemed to have come out of her shell a little and, as they rode out of the yard, she chattered away about the progress she had made with Spice and her hopes to compete in competition with him in the spring. He had had a lay-off for a couple of months and been turned out full-time with a small herd of geldings. He seemed to have filled out and gained confidence, and Karen told her that he was now better able to defend himself and hold his own against the other geldings if necessary.

Their ride was uneventful. They made their way up the hill and had a first canter at The Cutting, which Jenny found smooth enough but really rather slow. Barney's footfall felt heavy and lumbering in comparison to Daisy's nimble athleticism and, generally speaking, whilst he was sweet-natured and extremely obedient, Jenny found him a bit dull. When they returned to the yard, she had no desire to stay but felt obliged to untack him, give him a quick brush and make sure he was comfortable with plenty of hay and water before she took his tack back to the tack room to clean it. He lifted his head from his hay as she went towards the stable door to leave.

"Thank you, Barney," she said to him, moving towards him again to give him a good rub on his neck. She felt guilty at her own ingratitude and guilty that she did not feel more inclined to spend some time with him. She wondered if he was missing the attention from Carole and resolved to find some way to thank Carole for her kindness.

CHAPTER THIRTY-ONE

THE WEDDING

The following week Jenny found that she had no desire either to ride or to visit the yard, and she had to make a big effort to find enough to occupy her days. She had not realised until now how much time she had actually spent on her hobby: getting ready to go, riding, being at the yard, getting clean and dry again afterwards or reading about horses. Worse, she now found that there was little to occupy her thoughts either, now that she had no need to consult maps or plan her rides. She was at a loss as to know quite what to do next and was very glad that Tina's wedding was the following weekend so at least there was something different to look forward to. She knew that everyone from the yard would be there and was prepared for feeling a bit emotional, but hoped that she could pass it off with a joke that she always cried at weddings.

On the day of the wedding the weather was as near perfect as a dry, early January day could be, and Tina looked absolutely stunning in a fitted high-necked long-sleeved ivory silk gown with tiny covered buttons along the length of the back seam. Both Tina and her husband Adrian had large families, and they had broken with tradition to have two best men and two best ladies as well as ushers for the church.

The reception was a very jolly informal affair with all four of the best men and best ladies giving funny speeches, and many of the guests were crying with laughter by the time the speeches had finished. Tina and Adrian mingled with the guests after the wedding breakfast, and Jenny only had time for a very brief chat with Tina, who promised to call her very soon. There was a small dance floor and a DJ, and the party was in full swing until 2 a.m. Everyone, Jenny included, had a wonderful time, and the bride and groom had arranged for minibuses to take everyone home safely, so that no-one had to drive. It was almost 3 a.m. when Jenny put her key in the front door lock and waved goodbye to everyone still on the minibus.

When she awoke the following morning, the first thing to enter her head was a conversation she had had with a cousin of Adrian's. The family had farmed for many, many generations and owned several different farms within a radius of about fifty miles. The cousin, Ben, was interested in genealogy and had spent several years compiling the family tree – it had become a passion. He spoke with such enthusiasm on the subject that Jenny resolved to begin researching her own family tree first thing on Monday morning, at the records office in the nearest town. For the next six weeks, Jenny threw all her energy into her research and was extremely glad that she had found something which so totally absorbed her.

She also visited the yard each week to ride Barney for Carole and had warmed to him a little more. It was difficult not to, as he had such a sweet nature and not a mean bone in his body. He just wasn't very interesting and, for Jenny, there was simply no spark. She did however spend more time with him to give him some one-to-one attention – it was the least she could do for Carole, and Barney seemed to enjoy it. Wendy had suggested that Jenny join in a weekly group lesson in the indoor school and that she could ride Tallow, who seemed to be settling in nicely, but Jenny had no enthusiasm to do that and made her excuses about being busily involved in a family project, which in a manner of speaking was true.

She missed Daisy desperately, missed her quirky personality and her endearing ways. Jenny was often overcome with sadness at the thought of not having known Daisy for longer. Early mornings and bedtimes were the worst, when she had nothing else to occupy her thoughts, and it was at those times that she especially regretted having no visual memento to keep. Daisy had been so much more to her than just a horse to ride, she had been a best friend and a lifestyle, and an out-of-doors one at that.

Although Jenny loved the research and spent long hours at the records office and worked at home on her computer, she knew that once the warmer weather came she would hate to be indoors. One day when Wendy was on her own in the office, Jenny plucked up the courage to ask her if she had heard how Daisy was getting on.

Wendy immediately knew why she was asking and replied, "Very well, I believe, Jenny. She has settled in nicely. They had a few teething troubles with Daisy being a bit too lively, but they have now employed a groom to ride her three times a week while Felicity is at school and that seems to have taken the edge off her exuberance." She smiled ruefully and said, "It is a very different situation to Summer Camp Jenny, where Daisy had to contend with all the excitement of perhaps thirty children and thirty ponies on site, plus handlers she didn't know, different food, a different stable and a different routine. Horses like their routine and I never really thought for one moment that it would be difficult for her to settle at the Nugents, as long as there was a suitable routine for her."

"Well, I'm glad she's OK and has settled in nicely," Jenny said. It was almost true – she had not wanted Daisy to be miserable, of course not, but she had hoped that there might just be a tiny chance that Daisy would be a bit too lively or a bit too mischievous and perhaps the family might have second thoughts.

Tina emailed her every now and then with updates as to how the building work was progressing at the farm, and she seemed very happy with her new life. The barn and stables were finished and two outdoor arenas had been installed, at great expense, as they had had to use an outside contractor to lay the surface instead of doing the work themselves. There was a wash area where horses could be bathed, a purpose-built feed room and a rug room with two dryers, as well as an office and shower and toilet facility. Tina was still very keen on the idea of residential weekend workshops and had been busily decorating the large bedrooms in the farmhouse itself which was, for the most part, Elizabethan. She invited Jenny to stay for the first weekend in March and Jenny gratefully accepted, glad to have something different to think about and look forward to. She couldn't wait to see Tina again and catch up on all her news.

CHAPTER THIRTY-TWO
A WEEKEND WITH TINA

The first weekend in March was unusually warm for the time of year. Some of the spring flowers were already in bloom and there was a vivid sea of bright yellow daffodils to welcome Jenny as she turned off the road onto the long farm track. The farmhouse was an elegant, square building at the end of the track. A gravel drive swept around the farmhouse to the rear, and small rectangular lawns divided by rose beds surrounded the property on three sides. An old Victorian greenhouse stood against a grey stone wall which was covered in clematis, and Jenny thought it probably concealed a walled vegetable garden. As she stepped out of the car, Tina ran across the drive to meet her, threw her arms around her and gave her a big hug.

"I am so glad to see you!" she exclaimed excitedly. "You are my very first guest, Jenny. I can't wait to show you everything. Where is your bag? Come and say hello to Adrian, he's in the kitchen."

Tina led the way across one of the small lawns to a low wooden door which led into a large square room – formerly a cheese room, it now housed boots and coats and bicycles, as well as being a store for logs and a few tools. From there, another door led into the kitchen where Adrian was seated upon an old tapestry-covered sofa which he was sharing with three spaniels. In the centre of the room was an enormous square table which would easily seat sixteen or even twenty, Jenny thought. As Adrian rose to greet her, the dogs all leaped off the sofa at the same time and rushed towards Tina, jumping up excitedly. Like Tina, Adrian also gave Jenny a big hug, and she instantly felt at home.

"Welcome, Jenny! How are you? Tina has talked of nothing else all day. Come and sit down, the kettle's on. Tea or coffee?"

There was an Aga to one side of the kitchen and Jenny could easily imagine what a comfort that would be, to come downstairs to on a winter morning. Over a pot of tea and some homemade cake, both Tina and Adrian chatted enthusiastically about the problems they had resolved, the decisions they had made and their plans for the farm as a whole. The work was taking much longer than they had originally thought and there was still a great deal to do, but much of it was now cosmetic as the main building work had been finished. The farmhouse now benefitted from central heating, four new bathrooms and a laundry room, and would sleep its occupants plus twelve guests with ease. The attic floor had originally been servants' quarters and had been converted into some very pretty small bedrooms, with attic windows giving lovely views over both the parkland surrounding the house and the hills in the distance.

Tina had booked a table at the local pub for supper and they spent a very enjoyable evening together. Jenny met some of the locals who had known Adrian and his family for years, and they had lots of funny stories to tell about old times.

Towards the end of the evening, many of the locals left, and Tina, Adrian and Jenny moved to the big inglenook fireplace to enjoy a brandy nightcap.

Tina asked casually, "Are you riding much, Jenny?"

"No, not much," Jenny replied, then seeing Tina exchange a look with Adrian she hurriedly continued, "I ride Barney for Carole every week. I will, you know, do more – it's just a bit soon. I know I should ride lots of different horses, I know everyone says they are all special and if you are going to be a rider you should know that horses come and horses go and that's just life. I know that, but…" she bit her lip, "she was so special, you see, more of a lifestyle choice than a hobby. She meant the world to me. I have had dogs all my life and I have known some really intelligent animals and have always enjoyed that interaction, where both you and the animal can make yourselves understood without a common language, but Daisy… Daisy was something else. She was the best thing to happen to me in years."

Jenny knew the tears were about to flow and could do nothing to stop them, so she didn't even try. It was the first time she had cried since that awful day in Wendy's office when Mrs Nugent had wanted to take Daisy away earlier than planned. Tears streamed down her face in a torrent and she felt hot with embarrassment.

"Do excuse me," she mumbled, and fled to the ladies' room.

She had been sobbing in a cubicle for quite a little while before she heard the door open and close, then Tina's voice, "Jenny?"

Jenny felt a little silly and sheepishly opened the cubicle door and came out, dabbing her eyes and thinking that she must look a terrible sight.

"Sorry," she managed eventually, not knowing quite what else to say and feeling that the effort of talking might make her cry again.

Tina put both arms around her and held her tightly.

"Better out than in, that's what I say. No need to apologise. OK now?"

Jenny nodded. "Mmm, much better actually. Honestly. It's the first good cry I have had since she went."

Tina smiled.

"Time we went home, I think. How about a mug of cocoa and a ghost story in front of the fire?"

Adrian was an excellent storyteller, seemingly able to make up stories spontaneously, and it was past 1 a.m.

when the three of them eventually went off to bed. Jenny was occupying a delightful bedroom which overlooked the rear of the house, the new stables and the hills beyond. It was a fine dry night, with enough moonlight to illuminate the lawns and the rose beds beneath Jenny's window. The house was completely quiet and there was no sound from outside either; only the faint tick of a small clock in the bedroom kept Jenny company. She hoped that the ghost stories would not keep her awake, but the room was so cosy, her feather mattress so soft and she was so tired, that she fell asleep almost immediately.

Upon waking the following morning it took Jenny a moment or two to remember where she was. Tina had decorated each bedroom in a different style and for this one she had chosen pine furniture, floral wallpaper and matching fabric for the curtains and lampshades. There was a pine rocking chair with lace-trimmed cushions in one corner and a large brightly coloured rug upon the varnished wooden floor. The en-suite bathroom actually served two bedrooms, each of which had an adjoining door with a lock, and the bathroom was beautifully equipped with a state-of-the-art power shower, a heated towel rail and even a fitted hairdryer and heated mirror.

It was only 8 a.m. and Tina had said they would meet for breakfast at 9 a.m., so Jenny was able to take her time. Tina was already in the kitchen and had laid cereal, fruit juice and coffee at one end of the very large table.

"Good morning!" Tina greeted her when she arrived. "Perfect timing. Did you sleep well?"

"Like a top!" replied Jenny. "The bed is so comfortable, the room fabulous and I absolutely love your shower."

"We're going to sleep in each bedroom in turn so that we know what they are all like," said Tina. "If you can think of anything we have missed, or have any suggestions, do please say. Would you like anything cooked for breakfast?"

"No, thank you," said Jenny. "Cereal and coffee is perfect for me. Have you had yours?"

"Adrian left early and he always has something hot so I had mine with him," replied Tina, "but I'm always ready for another coffee, so I'll join you. I am dying to show you around!"

"I can't wait to see it all!" said Jenny with enthusiasm. "Tell me more about your plans."

The girls sat and chatted over their coffee and Tina outlined some of her ideas for her new venture. She intended to hire out one of the outdoor arenas by the hour, as there were people in the area who had horses at home but had to take them to a riding stable for lessons because they had no arena of their own. Some of the local event riders had their own tutors whom they preferred to use, and there were plenty of people who might like to hire an arena to practise in between their lessons.

Then there were the residential weekend workshops. Tina was going to advertise so that anyone with a specialist interest could hire the site, together with accommodation, arenas and stabling, and she would provide whatever additional services they required. She could also arrange workshops of her own, perhaps jumping clinics or something similar. In the short-term they could use some of the grazing land as a cross-country course and, again, hire it out or let people use it for practice or lessons for a fee. They had built twelve new wooden stables which Tina had nicknamed 'the wooden yard'.

Adrian had earmarked a large barn, within which he would build another twelve stables, so that Tina could offer residential workshops with accommodation for both riders and their horses. Adrian was an arable farmer, but there was enough grazing land for Tina to be able to have approximately twenty horses on site and to be able to let half the paddocks rest at any one time. There was nothing worse than not having sufficient grazing, she said, especially if horses were going to live out during the summer months.

She was gradually acquiring a small string of horses and ponies, not all of which had yet arrived, so they could offer hacks around the beautiful countryside and perhaps lessons as well. For the time being, the three new horses, and Archie, her own elderly gelding, were living out. Jenny could see how excited her friend was and was extremely pleased for her and hoped that her plans would turn out well.

"Come on!" said Tina when they had finished their coffee. "Come and have a look around and meet some of the new residents. We can take the dogs with us at the same time."

The dogs had been fast asleep until now, but the minute Tina stood up they were out of their beds and at the door in a flash, tails wagging expectantly. Tina chose boots and coats for both herself and Jenny from a selection in the former cheese room and they headed out to the paddocks so that Jenny could get an idea of the layout and extent of the site.

From the far side of the grounds the farm looked amazing, the house standing proudly to one side with some very large mature trees around it. There had been many renovations to the farmhouse over the years but it still bore some of the original features, in particular the beautiful mullioned windows. There were two horses and one pony grazing in the paddock and they seemed unconcerned about either the dogs or Tina and Jenny as they walked all around the perimeter of the first paddock.

Next stop was the barn which was to be fitted with new indoor stabling. The barn gave access to a small yard which was enclosed by wooden fencing and had a gate with which to access one of the arenas. *A useful waiting area if there is a competition and a queue for horses waiting to practise in the arena*, thought Jenny, having witnessed the arrangements for Wendy's recent gymkhana. The second arena was larger and had two gates, so that one horse could arrive as another was leaving, and it had a lovely aspect, slightly elevated and overlooking the paddocks. From there, Tina led Jenny to the wash area, which she was obviously very proud of. It was well drained and would have both cold and hot water supply. *No boiling of kettles on a cold day*, thought Jenny, as she remembered having to sponge Daisy down when she was covered in sweat after their run-in with the drag hunt.

Chapter Thirty-Three

Tina's Secret

The new wooden stables were in a self-contained inner yard with a water supply and tying-up area at one end, and the other end conveniently gave access to the rug room and tack room. There were six stables on either side of a wide central area so that the occupants could look across at one another, and the overall effect was quite cosy. They stopped at the very first stable for Jenny to meet Archie, Tina's horse. He was now retired, she said, but she had had him from a foal and he had been her very first equine love. She went on to explain.

"The truth is, I adore him and couldn't bear to part with him. He has lived with my aunt all these years until I had a place of my own to keep him. I didn't want to take him with me to lots of different yards as I moved around for work – it would have been too unsettling for him."

A recent memory flitted into Jenny's head and it took her a moment or two to remember the words, then she said to Tina, "You once told me that everyone remembers their first horse. You didn't tell me you still had yours!"

"Errr no," said Tina, looking a little sheepish. "I was—"

She was about to say something else when there was a noise behind them. It was a noise Jenny had not heard for a few weeks, one of her favourite noises of all time – it was the soft deep nickering sound that Daisy used to make. Jenny turned around to look behind her and see where it was coming from, and there, in the wooden stable opposite Archie's, was Daisy, her head over the stable door.

Jenny was too shocked to speak and stood there with her mouth open, staring at Daisy watching her from across the yard.

"Aren't you going to say hello?" asked Tina, who was grinning like a Cheshire cat.

"Yes… I… What is…? How did…? Is she…?" Jenny began, as she walked across to the stable where Daisy was standing. Upon reaching it, she opened the stable door and stepped inside, threw her arms around Daisy's neck and hugged her. Tears streamed down Jenny's face and she wiped them away with her hand.

"I don't know what to say," she said. "It's so good to see her! Why is she here? Are you looking after her for Mrs Nugent? How long is she here for? Can I come and see her? I don't understand, Tina, tell me! Please!"

"Well," said Tina, still beaming from ear to ear. "She no longer belongs to Mrs Nugent – they had to get rid of her."

"But why?" asked Jenny in amazement. "Wendy told me she had settled in really well."

"She had," said Tina, "she was doing very well indeed – until the pigs arrived."

"Pigs?" said Jenny in amazement. "What pigs?"

"Felicity's older brother Jeremy is at the agricultural college; he is passionate about organic farming and conservation, always has been, and he wants to make it his profession. He was given a grant to help with a programme of breeding certain farm animals which are in danger of becoming extinct, and one of his passions is rare pigs. Part of the reason for the family's move of house was so that they would have the land for him to use.

"One afternoon, Felicity went to tack Daisy up and take her out for a ride, and Daisy was behaving very strangely – she kept shaking her head, refused to leave her stable and was really quite stroppy about it. Felicity was quite frightened, so she went to get her mother, and Mrs Nugent then tried to get Daisy to leave the stable but Daisy was shaking like a jelly, and when they tried to pull her out she reared up. Mrs Nugent thought she was acting so strangely that it might be some kind of fit she was having, so they called the equine vet. To cut a long story short, the vet arrived and asked lots of questions and they eventually deduced that the arrival of the pigs, which were in sight of Daisy's stable, had coincided with this odd behaviour.

"There was nowhere else for the Nugents to keep Daisy and the pigs definitely had to stay, so Daisy had to go. The vet thought that getting rid of her was a bit extreme and suggested that they give her time to get used to the pigs, but Mrs Nugent was adamant that a horse which got in such a state when it was afraid of something was no use for children and especially not any use for Felicity to hack out on her own."

"Didn't they know she was afraid of pigs?" asked Jenny, her eyes wide.

"No," said Tina, "how could they? You know that and so do I, but I doubt if Wendy does or indeed anyone else."

Jenny's heart skipped a beat. "So… is she going back to Wendy?" she asked expectantly.

"No, Wendy doesn't know she's here and neither does Mrs Nugent."

"Why not?" asked Jenny, beginning to feel slightly confused.

"Because she belongs to someone else now, that's why," explained Tina.

Jenny's heart slipped right back down to her boots. "Oh, I just thought if Wendy had her back, I might get to ride her again, that's all," she said, feeling desolate with disappointment.

"Well, the new owner might let you ride her if you ask them nicely," said Tina.

"Would they?" said Jenny, instantly feeling optimistic again. "How do you know? Do you know them?"

"Oh yes," said Tina, her grin widening again, "and so do you."

"I do?" said Jenny. "Whoever is it, then?"

"Me!" said Tina with great satisfaction.

CHAPTER THIRTY-FOUR
THE WATER TROUGH

"You?! How, Tina? How have you come to own her? Why doesn't Mrs Nugent know you have her here? I just don't understand!" said Jenny, shaking her head in disbelief.

"Well, Mrs Nugent asked the equine vet if he knew anyone who might take Daisy, since she clearly couldn't stay where she was any longer. Adrian's cousin Cathy is an equine veterinary assistant with the same vet's practice and, quite by chance, she was with the vet on the visit. She knew I was looking for reliable horses which were free to a good home, and she had promised she would let me know if she heard of any. So she piped up and said she might know someone who could find Daisy a home and she could telephone them right away. If it was all OK, Daisy could spend the night at the vet's and be collected the following morning.

"Cathy messaged me straight away to give me some brief details of the mare, and she knew it had been vetted by her boss before Mrs Nugent purchased it, so she was confident that it was sound. So of course, I said yes, I would be happy to take it. The vet sedated Daisy sufficiently for them to load her onto a trailer, and Mrs Nugent took her to the vet's for the night where they kept an eye on her. I went to meet Cathy and collect the mare the following morning and I couldn't believe my eyes when I saw that it was Daisy. That was when Cathy told me the whole story about the pigs. Mrs Nugent hadn't asked to be told what happened to Daisy; she obviously trusted the vet, whom she has known for years, not to let Daisy go to anyone unsuitable."

"And Mrs Nugent really doesn't want her back?" asked Jenny, beginning to feel remarkably cheerful, more cheerful in fact than she had felt in months.

"No, certainly not, unless Jeremy forgets all about his passion for breeding rare pigs. The Nugents need a horse which doesn't mind other farm animals, especially pigs."

"Pigs!" exclaimed Jenny. "Pigs! I can't believe it! Of all the things to happen to bring her back to me. Pigs!" She began to laugh, and laughed so much that tears ran down her face.

Tina watched her, still grinning from ear to ear, thrilled to see the obvious joy her friend was feeling after so many tears.

"I have been dying to tell you but I wanted it to be a complete surprise. I don't suppose you have any riding clothes with you?" she asked.

"Not a thing," replied Jenny.

"Well, I have jods you could borrow, but I don't have a hat or boots which will fit you, unfortunately," said Tina apologetically. "Otherwise, we could have had a hack out."

"I'm just so thrilled to see her again," said Jenny. "Knowing that she is here and that I will be able to ride her again means the world to me. Thank you so much, Tina, I will forever be grateful."

"Well, you can make yourself useful by turning her out if you like," said Tina. "Until now, she has been taking a turn in the main paddock when it's empty; all the other horses are geldings and it seems best to keep them separate. Adrian has finished fencing the new paddocks and she can have one next to the boys now so that she can go out at the same time. They will be company for her over the fence until we have other mares to join her. It will be a treat, as she has been stabled quite a bit over the last two weeks. The paddock at the Nugents was very small and she wasn't out much because it was wet. She has never seen the new paddock so it will be a first for you both!"

"I would love to!" said Jenny enthusiastically. "Shall I do that now?"

"By all means," replied Tina. "I'll turn Archie out at the same time; he only stayed in to keep her company on the yard. I will show you where Daisy has to go."

Jenny fastened Daisy's head collar on with great satisfaction; she had really missed such simple little tasks over the past couple of months. Tina led Archie out of his stable and together they all walked around the back of the wooden yard and along a narrow track which led to another at right angles. There were four paddock gates leading off the track, two on the left and two on the right. Tina turned Archie out into the first paddock with the other geldings, and he cantered off to join his chums who had all lifted their heads to look at Daisy.

"She will be very much Queen Bee for a while," said Tina. "I hope she knows how to behave in the company of gentlemen! Her paddock is next on the left, Jenny. Take your time. I'll go back and begin mucking out their stables."

Jenny walked Daisy a little further on to her own paddock gate. It was new, as was all the fencing, and it looked very smart. It was a pleasure to open a gate which was properly balanced upon it's hinges and easy to open and close for a change! Daisy was looking over at the geldings with interest, but once they were inside the gate and Jenny had taken off her head collar she stayed close. Jenny wasn't sure why – was Daisy expecting her to stay as there were no other mares in the paddock? She decided to walk around the paddock to familiarise herself with it, and then saw the water trough.

"Let's go and have a drink, Daisy, you often used to do that first when I turned you out at Wendy's," she said.

The grass looked fabulous for grazing; but as Jenny walked diagonally across the paddock, Daisy made no attempt to drop her head and begin to graze, instead continuing to walk politely at Jenny's side. When they reached the trough, which was also brand new, Jenny waved a hand towards it and said, "Go on, Daisy, have a drink. It looks lovely and clean and fresh."

Daisy remained standing. She looked directly at Jenny, then at the trough, then at Jenny a second time. She nickered very softly.

Jenny suddenly realised what Daisy was doing – she was deferring to Jenny as herd leader and waiting for her to drink from the new water source first. *Oh my goodness*, she thought to herself, *I had better show her I understand*. She walked up to the trough and swished her hand in the water, enjoying the feel of the clear cool water against her skin. Then she bent her head towards the water a little as if to simulate drinking, straightened up again, turned away from the trough and walked past Daisy without looking at her. Once she had passed Daisy's rump she turned to face the trough again. Daisy promptly walked forwards and had a lovely long drink, then turned away from Jenny and the trough, with water still pouring from her lips, dropped her head and began to graze. Jenny smiled. *What a lovely sight*, she thought to herself, *my beautiful Daisy, in the sunshine, in a lovely clean paddock, safe, well fed, well looked after and, most of all, free to be my friend again*. She turned to walk back across the paddock to go and help Tina on the wooden yard.

Chapter Thirty-Five

Catch Me If You Can

When Jenny went to get Daisy in for tea, it was a different story. Gone was the well-mannered deferential mare of that morning. The new Daisy had no intention of leaving such a fabulous new paddock, only to be brought in to spend yet more time in a stable!

Tina was greatly amused at Daisy's antics and called out to Jenny, "I'll carry on with getting the boys in and come and give you a hand when I've finished, if you need it."

Jenny stood still and thought for a moment. She had seen other clients run around after horses which did not want to be caught, and there had been occasions when two or more staff at Wendy's stable yard had had to join forces to catch one, usually because the horse was new to the yard and not yet in a routine. This was a first though, and Jenny knew it was very important for her to find an immediate solution and set a precedent straight away, in case Daisy decided this was a wonderful new game which could be played every day of the week. She had approached Daisy twice so far, and each time Daisy had shaken her head from side to side and actually stamped her right foreleg as well, as if to emphasise no. Then she'd cantered right across the paddock to the opposite corner, as far away as she could.

There has to be another way, thought Jenny, as she walked across the paddock at a normal pace without rushing. She could see that Daisy was watching her, but her head was still down and she had not stopped grazing.

When Jenny was about thirty metres away, she held the head collar and lead rope out at arm's length for several seconds, until she was sure Daisy had seen them, then dropped them onto the grass. As she continued to walk slowly towards Daisy, she held both arms out from her sides to demonstrate that she wasn't holding anything. Daisy lifted her head to look at her, and Jenny thought to herself, *Ah, I have her attention! Oh good, I wasn't expecting that!*

When she reached Daisy she gave her a good rub along her neck and patted her.

"Can we talk about this?" Jenny asked. "It's nearly teatime. You want your tea, don't you?"

She patted Daisy's neck again, but this time kept her hand there instead of removing it.

"Everyone else is coming in for the night, Daisy, and you will be out here all on your own if you don't come in. I promise you can come back out in the morning along with everyone else. Now then, shall we go and find the head collar? Come on."

Jenny turned to walk away and looked back at Daisy over her shoulder. "Come on," she repeated, and remained still with her back to Daisy and looking straight ahead. To her relief, Daisy took a step forward, and Jenny gave her a big pat and they continued to walk together, back to the head collar. When they reached it Daisy stood and waited patiently for Jenny to put it on and made no attempt to canter off again. Jenny hugged her.

"Good girl!" she said emphatically, giving her a good rub. "Good girl!"

Tina looked up from cleaning Archie's feet as Jenny walked Daisy onto the wooden yard.

"That's a surprise!" she said. "That looked like it was going to be a long job. I thought I might be able to sell tickets." She grinned and turned her attention back to Archie.

"We just needed to have a little chat, that was all," replied Jenny primly. "A lady has a right to an opinion, you know." She threw Tina a glance and grinned back. "I tell you what though, Tina, she was so adamant she wasn't coming in that when she shook her head to say no she even stamped her foot! It did look funny."

"Ah yes," said Tina, "I meant to tell you about that. It's a very funny new habit she acquired at the Nugents. I don't know quite how – I expect she saw someone else do it and she is copying their action."

"She should be on the stage," said Jenny. "I remember a television series from my childhood where there was a horse which did funny things like that. We could make some money out of her! How do you fancy getting a job, Daisy?"

Jenny thoroughly enjoyed her weekend at Tina's and they agreed that Jenny would now spend as much time as she could at the farm.

Tina had said to her, "Daisy cost me nothing, and if you care for her and pay for her feed, shoes and insurance, I have no need to charge you for livery. You will save me money anyway, by giving your time for free and helping me with the running of the yard."

Firstly, however, Jenny wanted to go and see Wendy to explain what had happened, and she also wanted to speak to Carole. Wendy was absolutely delighted for her and gave her a big hug.

"I am so glad, Jenny. I felt so rotten selling her like that. I'm really sorry it didn't work out for Felicity and her family, but Felicity still has lessons here and I can offer them another horse which will be much more suitable for their needs, so it has ended well for everyone. I'll telephone Carole and pass on your message and tell her that you're happy to continue to ride Barney until she can make other arrangements."

As Jenny drove away from Wendy's yard she felt more lighthearted than she had done for months and stopped at the tack shop on the way home to stock up on Daisy's favourite meadow-herb treats. There were lots of new clothes on display for the spring season and some lovely lighter-weight rugs for horses, and she was very keen to do some shopping for both herself and Daisy! First though, she would have to have a stocktake and discuss with Tina what Daisy actually needed most.

The next few weeks were an absolute delight for Jenny – she could treat Daisy as her own horse again and she enjoyed every second of their time together. She spent a great deal of time at the farm and visited every day, relishing the experience of being in the fresh air all day again. The clocks had changed and evenings were lighter, so the horses did not need to come in so early. She helped with the mucking out and preparing the feeds, skipped out the paddocks to keep them fresh and swept the yard on windy days when the straw blew all around.

She printed some maps of the area and began exploring in the same way she had when she first started to hack out on her own, colouring the tracks on the map with yellow highlighter pen when she had ridden them and gradually extending the routes. Tina was unable to join them very often as there was still much to be done, but when she did she was both grateful for and impressed by Jenny's ability to share her detailed knowledge of the area. It was exciting to be seeing new territory for the first time and, since Tina had never ridden the area and did not know it very well at all, Jenny was able to tell her about difficult gateways, broken fences and various obstacles to easy hacking.

She took photographs of various things on her phone while she was out and made a note of the location on her map so that Adrian was able to effect repairs quite quickly.

Chapter Thirty-Six
New Challenges

Tina was initially a little concerned that Daisy was not familiar with the area either and had said to Jenny, "Please have your phone with you always. I do sometimes worry about you being a long way off and out there all on your own."

And Jenny had replied, "I'm not on my own, I'm with Daisy."

There were, of course, many things that they came across for the first time ever, and Daisy found them frightening. Jenny was often surprised that things which looked extremely scary didn't bother Daisy one bit, yet the oddest things could cause Daisy to snort, panic and flee without warning and take Jenny completely by surprise. Such a thing was a large box of carrots. The men were harvesting vegetables in the fields, and the carrots which had been collected were stacked in boxes at the end of one of the rows. Daisy was absolutely terrified of them and it took six attempts to get her past the carrots in a reasonably orderly manner. Eventually, Jenny had to settle for a sort of rapid sideways trot while Daisy kept her eyes on the carrots the whole time. The men, meanwhile, thought it all hilarious and cheered and applauded when Jenny finally went by.

Jenny thought that a consistent approach was best and she developed a routine for dealing with the problem of scary objects. The minute Daisy balked at something, Jenny would talk to her and encourage her to stop and look at it, at the same time loosening the rein to indicate that she did not think Daisy needed to be tightly controlled. Then she would give Daisy a pat, give her time to consider the obstacle and ask her to go forward a pace or two. If she complied, Jenny would halt her again and praise her, relax the rein further and let Daisy stand for a few seconds more. Sometimes, if it was possible, they would actually stop next to the item and Jenny would let Daisy sniff it and have a proper look.

On one occasion they came across two gentlemen on motorbikes. Jenny had heard the noise from about a kilometre away and had kept talking to Daisy all the way there, partly to maintain a 'connection' with her and partly to give her something else to think about in case the sound scared her. When the motorcyclists saw them approach they stopped the bikes and turned their engines off.

Jenny halted Daisy and sat with a relaxed rein and chatted to the men for a few moments, to show Daisy there was nothing to be scared of. Then she said, "Would you mind if my horse came closer to have a look?"

"By all means, miss," said one of the men, "but my mate here is as afraid of horses as your horse is of his bike."

Jenny laughed and reassured them that Daisy was perfectly friendly and wouldn't hurt anyone, so one of the men made a fuss of her as she inspected his bike very closely. The other man then felt able to join in and even offered Daisy a mint. The men suggested that Jenny might like to move on before they put their helmets on and started their engines once more, but they had been such a good introduction for Daisy that Jenny decided to stay. She moved back a little way instead and sat, patting Daisy and talking to her. Sure enough, Daisy was sufficiently relaxed and comfortable with the gentlemen that neither the helmets nor the engines starting up worried her now. Jenny was really pleased and hoped that the next time she and Daisy encountered motorbikes, Daisy would remember this very pleasant introduction to them.

There was also new wildlife to introduce Daisy to. There was a lot more woodland in this area than they had found at Wendy's and, consequently, a great many deer, together with badgers, hares, rabbits, hawks, buzzards and pheasants. The pheasants were the scariest – they made such a terrible noise as they flew up suddenly in front of Daisy's hooves, and they even startled Jenny once or twice. Pheasant chicks were being raised in one area of woodland and Jenny was very careful to whisper to Daisy and keep very quiet when they walked past. Daisy seemed to understand Jenny's whispered verbal command "Quietly, Daisy," and would promptly slow down her pace and place her feet very slowly and deliberately as if she were tiptoeing.

They rode through the wood one morning very early and found there were cobwebs covered in dewdrops all over the trees and bushes. The sun was beginning to shine through the branches of the trees, and the dewdrops looked like tiny jewels sparkling on silken threads. The wood was silent, without even birdsong, and the clearing had a quite magical air about it. There were no signs anywhere to indicate that Jenny was trespassing, and she sincerely hoped she was not, for she had no desire to upset Tina and Adrian's neighbours. However, on one occasion she heard a tractor coming and thought it best to get out of sight so, after whispering "Quietly, Daisy," she pushed Daisy through the bushes into a tiny clearing behind a large tree trunk and they stayed very still and quiet while the tractor went past. As Daisy stood behind the foliage waiting for the tractor to go, Jenny stifled giggles, greatly amused by the thought that Daisy seemed to understand that they were hiding and didn't move a muscle!

Daisy had initially been quite startled by the propane gas bird-scarer guns which Adrian used to keep the birds off his crops, but they sometimes continued firing through the night, and before long she didn't react at all, even when they were very close to one when it went off. The woods were full of deer and they were often seen around the arable fields. Jenny thought that the deer must also be oblivious to both scarecrows and bird-scarers as they heard them so often.

There were certain places on their hacks where Jenny knew that Daisy considered the next hundred yards or so her personal racetrack. Jenny, meanwhile, was determined that any cantering Daisy did would be on Jenny's command and not because Daisy took her completely by surprise. Trying to pre-empt Daisy and keep her under control was at times nigh on impossible. On some occasions, Jenny found that Daisy was deliberately being terribly good and, Jenny felt, actually pretending that she had no intention of getting up to any mischief, and then –Wham! – with a skip she would charge off and gallop like a rocket. One of her favourite places to do this was dotted with bushes and resembled a slalom course; it took all of Jenny's concentration to ride it, and when they were going so fast she didn't like to distract Daisy from concentrating lest they had an accident. One morning it was actually frosty and Jenny had not intended to canter at all, thinking that the ground was far too slippery. The cold weather seemed to have livened Daisy up, however, and on that particular morning, when she suddenly took off with Jenny in the most inappropriate place, Jenny's attempt at taking back control was met with Daisy dropping her head down very low and putting in a huge buck!

In the main, though, Daisy was incredibly well-behaved and trustworthy. One day they were heading towards a particularly nice canter and had just left a stony track and were about to turn a corner onto a lovely flat grass field about 500 metres long. It was a warm mid-morning, with clear blue sky and sunshine, and the field was very sheltered. As Daisy stepped onto the grass she pulled up sharply and drew back. In the field were about twenty deer, lying down and sunbathing. At the sight of Daisy, most of them got up, and Jenny said to her, "They aren't afraid of us, Daisy, so let's go!" and as they set off at a canter the deer joined them. It was the most magical experience, to be cantering all the way up the field in the middle of a herd of deer. The deer, of course, could smell and see a horse and presumably thought Jenny was a part of it and therefore not any kind of threat. When Daisy and Jenny finished their canter the deer carried on and bounded off into the woods.

CHAPTER THIRTY-SEVEN
AN UNUSUAL TREAT

There were also new experiences to be had back at the yard. Jenny fixed a chain across Daisy's stable door so that she could have her door pinned open and enjoy the sunshine streaming into her stable. It was so much easier and quicker for Jenny to duck underneath the chain than to keep opening and closing and bolting the door every time she wanted to go in or out. Most mornings, she sat underneath the chain with her legs stretched out into the yard to have her coffee and share an apple with Daisy. Sometimes, since Daisy was a real sun worshipper, she would stand behind Jenny with her nose directly above Jenny's head, her eyes closed and have a nap.

Daisy occasionally used this new-found freedom to be mischievous, and one day Jenny was crouching outside Daisy's stable, sweeping something into a dustpan. It had been raining and the yard was very wet, and Daisy reached forward over her chain to put her nose underneath Jenny's bottom and with one push tipped Jenny head-first into a puddle.

It was during one of the occasions when Jenny was enjoying her coffee that she discovered something which instantly became the fifth item on Daisy's list of favourite things. Jenny had forgotten her apple, but she did not want to disappoint Daisy, who was by now used to a post-hack treat and she herself was hungry too. She knew that Tina kept biscuits in a tin in the tack room where the kettle and mugs were and discovered to her delight that the tin contained a packet of peanut and honey cereal bars, Tina's favourites. Jenny took one and was both surprised and greatly amused by Daisy's reaction to her half-share. First she lifted her lips and parted them in the way she signified a taste or smell she liked or something which amused her. Secondly, she began to nudge Jenny, quite forcibly, around her pockets, obviously wanting to know if there were any more!

"Stop it, Daisy!" said Jenny, laughing at her antics.

The next day, Jenny remembered her apple as usual and to her great amusement found that once Daisy had eaten her half-share she began to investigate Jenny's pockets again, obviously hoping that they contained another cereal bar. The cereal bars became a regular feature of their daily life, and Daisy's obsession with them amused a great many people over the next few months. If Daisy didn't want to do something, Jenny only had to use the words, 'You can have a cereal bar if you're good,' and the result was instant co-operation.

On one occasion it almost ended in disaster. Daisy had often watched Jenny fetch a cereal bar from the tack room, and one day, when Daisy was tethered outside her stable while Jenny went off the yard to find something, Daisy managed to untie herself and walked into the tack room to go and find the cereal bars for herself. Jenny came back just in time to see Daisy's thick white tail disappearing through the tack room door. She had great difficulty getting Daisy to reverse out again, as there were saddles on racks to either side of her and there was no room for her to turn round. In addition, Daisy seemed to have decided that, having found the very important tin, she was not leaving without sampling some of the contents!

The area was very popular with ramblers and walkers, and Daisy was an attractive horse as well as being friendly. People often admired her as she and Jenny passed by. Jenny had always been careful to ensure that both Daisy and her tack looked immaculate, and one of Daisy's best features was her beautiful long thick white tail. Jenny washed it first thing every morning while Daisy ate her breakfast and before they went out for their ride. With the aid of two buckets, one of soapy water and one of clear, Jenny was able to wash and rinse it in under a minute and she would then put a towel around it lengthways, fold it in half and secure the towel with some Velcro which she had stitched to one end.

By the time Daisy had finished her hay, the tail was dry, and it was permanently tangle-free. Its lushness drew comment from many a rambler or passer-by. Daisy adored attention and, regardless of Jenny's instructions, would turn off their path to head for any group of people, hoping for at least admiration and, at best, something tasty to eat. Daisy was well aware that where there were walkers and ramblers, there were rucksacks and lunchboxes, and many a walker went hungry because Daisy had fluttered her very long dark eyelashes in their direction and been rewarded with an entire apple or, on one occasion, a cheese sandwich.

Jenny was not too keen on the idea of Daisy eating cheese sandwiches and felt quite guilty about the ramblers giving up their food. One morning their ride took them past some engineers in vans, who were making repairs to the telephone network, and even Jenny was completely taken by surprise when Daisy suddenly stopped and put her head through the van's open window. The men were having their coffee and sharing a packet of biscuits and were at first taken aback but then most amused at suddenly being mugged by a horse!

Tina said to Jenny one morning, "I hear you met the telephone engineers."

"How an earth do you know that?" replied Jenny.

"Adrian was in the pub the other evening and the men were talking about a horse suddenly putting its head through the van window and wanting their biscuits," said

Tina. "Adrian asked them what colour it was so we knew it was Daisy. Has she no shame?"

"No," replied Jenny, "none at all unfortunately."

Tina laughed. "Changing the subject, I have the horse dentist coming this afternoon to see the others; would you like him to check her at the same time? I recall that she was quite frightened by the dentist when he came to Wendy's, so she may be difficult. I have warned him."

"I'm not too keen on the dentist myself," said Jenny, "so I think I can understand!"

The horses were all brought into their stables before the dentist arrived, and Jenny needn't have worried. The dentist was young and extremely good-looking, tall and dark with a lovely smile. He smelled of lavender oil – presumably to calm nervous horses – and on the basis of getting the most potentially difficult patient out of the way, he visited Daisy first. Upon walking into the stable he greeted her with, "Hello, gorgeous, open up for me please, darling."

And to Jenny's astonishment, Daisy relaxed instantly and took to him straight away. She stood like a lamb for him, and within a few minutes he had pulled out a wolf tooth which he said might have been giving her a little trouble!

"I wish he were my dentist!" said Jenny to Tina later.

CHAPTER THIRTY-EIGHT
TEDDY HAS A PROBLEM

One morning Tina said to Jenny, "Guess who telephoned me last night." Jenny shook her head. Tina went on, "Do you remember glamour-boy Teddy? Well, his owner has been keeping him at Wendy's until now and he has had a few problems. He seems to find the constant activity and bustle of a busy yard stressful, and to make matters worse he won't go out in the paddock."

"Won't go out?" said Jenny in astonishment. "Do you mean he won't leave his stable?"

Tina shook her head. "They take him out of his stable

and put him in the paddock, but he simply won't socialise or graze. He stands at the paddock gate, literally all day if necessary, until they bring him in again, by which time, apart from anything else, he's hungry and he hasn't moved a muscle to keep warm. Obviously they can't leave him out there for too long to get cold and hungry, but they've tried all sorts of things and Wendy has run out of ideas. She asked me if I would have him here, to see if a really quiet yard would be more suitable for him. I think I told you, he had very little turnout where he originally came from; the horses were stabled all the time apart from exercise so he simply isn't used to it."

"Poor Teddy!" said Jenny sympathetically. "I can't imagine being a horse and being in a stable all day every day, never having the sun on your back or a roll or a romp with your chums in the paddock."

"His owner came to see me this morning to have a look round and she thinks it's worth a try," said Tina excitedly. "He will be my very first livery client, Jenny! They're arriving at 11 a.m. Are you hacking this morning?"

"I was going to," said Jenny, "but we have done quite a lot this week. I could give Daisy half an hour in school for a change. I would love to be here to see him arrive."

At just past 11 a.m., Wendy's two-horse trailer drove up the track leading to the farm, followed by a 4 x 4 driven by Teddy's owner, Samantha. Adrian, Tina and Jenny had been in the kitchen for half an hour, having coffee and excitedly waiting for the new arrival. They went straight out to the yard to greet Wendy and Samantha and show them where to park.

"Gosh, this is nice!" said Wendy appreciatively, giving Tina a hug.

"I'll show you round properly when we have Teddy unloaded, if you have time," said Tina. Samantha had already parked her car and was at the back of the trailer, lowering the door.

Teddy had lost none of his film-star glamour and looked just as Jenny remembered him. He reversed off the trailer with ease and stood at Samantha's side, his head up, looking around him with interest. *He moves like a model,* thought Jenny, *so graceful and elegant, such a deliberate walk.*

They made their way to the wooden yard where Archie had been brought in to keep Teddy company initially. Teddy's stable was next to Daisy's so that he could look across at Archie. Tina made sure Teddy was comfortable and they decided to leave him with Archie for half an hour while they all had coffee together.

Jenny was pleased to see Wendy again and they chatted about Jenny's progress with Daisy, while Adrian, Tina and Samantha discussed how best to deal with Teddy. They agreed that he should stay in his stable for the rest of the day. Samantha would put all her tack and belongings into the tack room and rug room and stay for an hour or so in case there was a problem. Providing Teddy seemed happy enough, she would come back the following morning. If the weather was fine they would try putting Teddy in the paddock with the other geldings to see how he got on. The paddocks were quite private and quiet, and Tina quietly hoped that Teddy might eventually get the message and mingle with the others and graze normally.

After Tina had shown Wendy around, Wendy said her goodbyes and promised to return very soon and have lunch with them. Jenny cleaned her tack in the sunshine and chatted to Samantha, whose main interest was dressage. She had hacked a little, but was not keen on wind and rain and was not at heart really a country girl. She adored riding in school though, loved dressage and had achieved high standards. She was really looking forward to using the school for the first time once Teddy had settled in.

The following morning Jenny went out to hack on Daisy as usual, and when she returned and turned Daisy out she was dismayed to see that Teddy was standing at the gate of the geldings' paddock, well away from the others. It was a beautiful day and Daisy stopped and looked at Teddy as they made their way down the track to turn her out.

"It's a terrible shame, Daisy," Jenny said to her; "all this lovely grass and lovely sunshine and he wants to go back inside!"

Daisy, of course, once free, made a beeline for her water trough then dropped her head to graze. Jenny stood and watched her for a little while, occasionally glancing at Teddy who didn't move at all. On her way back to the yard she stopped to pat him and have a chat. He continued to look in the direction of his stable the whole time. Tina was out for the afternoon and Jenny had promised to keep an eye on Teddy and to telephone Tina if there was a problem. They had agreed that they would not rush to bring Teddy in, unless he seemed distressed or anxious; the weather was warm and dry and the other geldings were friendly enough.

Jenny went back to the paddocks at frequent intervals, and on each occasion Teddy was still in the same place. Three hours later, she went to look again and was thrilled this time to see that he had actually moved! Not very far, admittedly, but he was about a quarter of the way down the paddock, standing at the fence between Daisy's paddock and the geldings', and Daisy was standing directly opposite him on the other side of the fence, dozing. Jenny crept away and, about half an hour later, went to look again. Daisy was grazing in almost the same spot where she had previously been dozing, and Teddy had his head down grazing too, on the opposite side of the fence in the spot where he too had been previously standing. Half an hour later, Daisy was over on the other side of her paddock and Teddy had taken up his position at the gate again.

Jenny relayed the news to Tina when she returned.

"Well, it's progress of a sort, isn't it?" Tina said hopefully. "Maybe tomorrow he will venture a little further."

Samantha duly returned the next morning and put Teddy through his paces in the arena. Jenny watched and thought they both looked amazing. She did not know very much about dressage, but Samantha and Teddy made it look effortless. The movements were so precise and so graceful, and Samantha appeared to do absolutely nothing at all, although Jenny knew what hard work school was even if you were only learning to walk, trot and canter!

The girls had told Samantha about Teddy's movements on the previous afternoon, and it happened to be Daisy's day off, so she was already out. Jenny went with Samantha to turn Teddy out, and Daisy was already dozing by the fence line. Once free, Teddy looked all around for a few moments, but this time, instead of turning back and taking up his waiting position at the gate, he walked across to where Daisy was standing and stood opposite her – he didn't graze, he just stood there, facing in the same direction she was facing, with his back to the other geldings.

"Well, that's the most progress I've seen in six months!" said Samantha, obviously pleased.

CHAPTER THIRTY-NINE
TINA HAS AN IDEA

After a few days it became obvious that Teddy had no interest in being one of the boys. Jenny simply couldn't imagine him charging around the paddock on a windy day with the rest of the horses. She could now see how he managed to remain permanently spotlessly clean! He reminded her of a Noel Coward character in a film, elegant and immaculate in a silk smoking jacket and cravat, or a naval commander in a smart uniform, tall and dignified.

A week later Tina said to Jenny, "You can say no, but I have a favour to ask you. Do you think we might put Teddy in with Daisy? He is obviously comfortable with her, for whatever reason. He doesn't seem to have a mean streak and I cannot imagine him harming anything at all. Geldings and mares run quite happily together in herd situations, and I know of people who mix them in the paddock and it works beautifully. People also keep horses with cattle or sheep. Much depends upon the horses themselves, of course – a mean horse will be mean wherever it is. What do you think?"

"We could certainly try it," said Jenny. "Daisy seems to get on with *all* other horses, I have never known her not to, and if you and I are both here we would be able to intervene very quickly if there was a problem."

"Tomorrow morning, then," said Tina. "I'll tell Samantha and just make sure it is OK with her."

The following morning Teddy was put back in his stable after exercise to wait until Daisy came back from her hack, so that they could both go out at the same time. Jenny took the lead with Daisy and took her into her paddock but did not unclip her head collar. Samantha and Tina followed with Teddy. Once Teddy was also in Daisy's paddock, he simply stood there and looked straight ahead. Jenny unclipped Daisy, who took a step forward, turned and looked back at Teddy. Samantha unclipped him as well, but he didn't move. Daisy flattened her ears and tossed her head at him, before looking ahead again and sauntering off to the middle of the paddock where she dropped her head to graze.

"Well, you've been told, Teddy!" said Samantha with a grin as she stepped back. The girls turned back to the gate and let themselves out. Teddy, who had not yet moved, turned to look at the girls, then looked over at Daisy, then he too walked forwards, dropped his head and began to graze.

The weather turned unusually warm for a few days and Jenny began to notice that there were more flies in the paddock than usual. The horses swished their tails and shook their heads but the flies were extremely persistent. Jenny thought it must be incredibly annoying to have several flies walking around in different directions on your nose or back – it looked awful too.

She asked Tina if there was anything they could do to stop the horses from being pestered.

"Mmm, difficult," replied Tina. "I suppose if you don't want flies to annoy you, you shouldn't have been a horse. It's the same with cattle. Flies carry all sorts of disease and can be a real problem. There are lots of sprays and lotions and potions, some natural, some chemical. I always worry that the chemical ones will end up on the grass when it rains and then be eaten by the horses! I have known people spend a fortune on all sorts of things, even garlic supplements. Personally I have always preferred fly masks – those fringes you see horses wearing? At least they are user friendly. Have a look in the tack shop and see what you can find, Jenny. It depends on what you feel comfortable with and, more to the point, what Daisy prefers."

Jenny visited the tack shop on her way home and found that Tina was absolutely right, there was a bewildering array of products to choose from. She could not make her mind up between a net fly mask which covered the whole head and a traditional fringe, so she bought both. The following day she put the net mask on Daisy, who did not seem to mind at all, and Jenny wondered if the dark grey net also acted as sunglasses! After a day or two, though, she noticed that Daisy was constantly rubbing the side of her head and trying to get the net off. So the following morning, before she turned Daisy out, she held both the mask and the fringe out in front of her and let Daisy choose. Daisy gave a very gentle push to the hand holding the fringe, so Jenny used that. Each morning she repeated the process and Daisy chose the fringe every time.

Chapter Forty
Open Day

Tina and Adrian had planned to have a formal opening of the yard after Easter and they had scheduled a date in May in their diaries. They had thought long and hard about what form the Open Day should take as they wanted it to be something different. Jenny had been a party to most of the discussions and between them they had decided upon a games day, with three events: a Chase Me Charlie jumping competition, where riders who scored a clear round went on to the next one and, after each one, the height of the fences was raised; a cross-country jumping relay race, for which teams had to be drawn; and an obstacle course against the clock. A few local suppliers of horse feed, tack and outdoor clothing had agreed to set up stalls, and there were to be live demonstrations of farriery and equine physiotherapy at intervals throughout the day. The local publican had agreed to come and cook a barbecue lunch, and there were pastries and coffee at mid-morning, tea and cakes during the afternoon, and canned drinks and snacks throughout the day from a vending machine.

Neither Tina nor Adrian was very keen on admin or paperwork and neither had the necessary computer skills. They were immensely grateful to be able to hand over to Jenny, who established the office for them, bought and set up a computer system and mounted an enormous planning board on the wall. The board was covered in notes, Post-its and lists for the whole month. She put up a large sign on the door, 'The Operation Centre', and had taken charge of printing all the advertising material, programmes, entry forms and posters for the day itself. She had impressed both Tina and Adrian by hand-painting colourful signs to direct people to parking, toilets and showers, refreshments and the information tent. For the four weeks prior to the event she had spent every afternoon either on the telephone or on the computer. All the entrants had been informed in advance of their competitor number, team number and class times, to save time on the day, and there were sixty competitors in total.

They were lucky with the weather which was glorious for the whole week prior to the Open Day. The blossom on the fruit trees made the farmhouse look even more idyllic and the clematis was in full bloom. The yard looked impressive too, and the well-equipped indoor stables for visiting horses were already prepared with straw and water. For Tina, Adrian and Jenny the day began at 5 a.m. – the resident horses were all living out and needed to be checked before work on the Open Day started. The first lorries began to arrive at 7 a.m. and were directed by Adrian to the large field which he had mown and sectioned with ropes on the previous day, and by 9 a.m. the ground was teeming with people. Jenny had based herself in the information tent and was in contact with both Adrian and Tina via her mobile. Cathy, Adrian's cousin who was an equine veterinary assistant, had come to help them with any injuries or problems with the horses during the day, and she was also a qualified first-aider. It was 1 p.m. before Jenny and Tina met up for a thirty-minute lunch break.

"Gosh, this is full-on!" said Tina as she flopped down on a bench. "It's going well, though. The cross-country relay finished on time and everyone was really pleased with the course. Lots of people have said they will come back to use it to practise for their other competitions. The obstacle course will be easier this afternoon; I can see the whole course from my stand. And Chase Me Charlie will be a fun event to finish on as we have fewer competitors for that and it is always popular with spectators. I once watched it at a very grand horse trial. In the end, it was a jump-off between a hugely powerful showjumper and this really small horse which was half its size. There came a point when they dared not put the fence up any higher, so they decided that after every clear round the riders should remove an item of tack from the horse. Eventually, both riders were jumping without either bridles or saddles – it was amazing to watch. The showjumper won but everyone was rooting for the little one and they gave her a standing ovation. It was so exciting."

The afternoon events went as planned and, as it was such a fine day, many of the competitors stayed after their classes to have more refreshments, walk around the yard and look at the facilities, or just sit on the grass and chat with other riders. Some came into the information tent and asked Jenny questions about the facilities and what was planned for future events, and she was unable to close the information point until nearly 7 p.m.

It was almost 8:30 p.m. by the time everyone had gone, and the girls made their way back to the house and flopped onto the old sofa in the kitchen.

"Gosh, that was a long day!" said Tina. "I'm exhausted and I'm famished!"

Jenny laughed. "Me too," she said. "What shall we have for supper?"

"I'll text Adrian and see how long he is going to be," replied Tina. "I don't think I have the energy to cook – how about the pub?"

Adrian thought that going out for supper was a grand idea and said he would be home in about fifteen minutes and could meet them at the pub in half an hour. Tina telephoned to book a table for them and, after a really quick wash and brush up, they set off. The pub was crowded and very noisy but luckily their table was in a little room to one side of the bar.

"Do you think everyone had a good time today, Jenny? Was it a success, do you think?" asked Tina.

"I'm sure it was," Jenny replied. "Lots of people told me they had really enjoyed it, and the horses were all very well behaved, weren't they? I made some notes about what people asked me – we could do with a regular newsletter sent to email addresses, publicising jumping clinics, or cross-country practice days, and so on. The key to it all is in the organisation, I think. I was really pleased that everyone knew exactly where they had to be and what they had to do and we didn't have any unnecessary delays."

Tina nodded. "I have you to thank for that; your ability to plan things is remarkable. I have never seen such efficient list-making!" She grinned. "Thank you, Jenny, you've been a tower of strength these past four weeks. I didn't realise how much organisation would be needed and we couldn't have done it without you. We make a good team."

For a minute, Tina looked serious, and Jenny was just about to ask her if she was OK when Adrian arrived. He was keen to share his views on the day and he too was very pleased with how successful it had been.

Adrian disappeared to go and order their supper and buy another round of drinks, and Tina said to Jenny, "I've been thinking. We work really well together, Jenny, I like the way you handle the horses, you are an exceptionally good organiser and you get on really well with everyone. I have so many ideas for the business, but this week has shown me that I need a good second-in-command on site seven days a week. Daisy is happy here, and you already spend a great deal of time here during the week. You don't have to give me an answer this instant, but do you think you might consider coming to live here and working for me full-time as my manager? As part of the package of salary and perks I would sign Daisy over to you so that she would become yours once and for all. She cost me nothing, and I would love you to be able to call her your own after all you have been through. In a few months, if things worked out well, perhaps we could even consider a partnership."

"Goodness!" said Jenny. "I wasn't expecting that at all. I adore being here, love the outdoor lifestyle, love being around Daisy so much, but I would hate to let you down, Tina, you have been so good to me and you are a wonderful friend, so is Adrian. I have never held a management position before. It would be a huge responsibility, a big challenge."

"One you are more than capable of meeting," said Tina emphatically. "I promise you, I have given it a great deal of thought, Jenny. Adrian and I have discussed it a lot and he is entirely in favour. Please think it over, no pressure."

Adrian re-appeared at that moment.

"I've asked Jenny if she would consider coming to work with us and live on site," Tina said to him.

"She said yes I hope?" asked Adrian, raising his eyebrows.

"She's going to think about it. I told her there was no hurry," said Tina.

Adrian looked at Jenny and smiled. "We really would be thrilled to have you with us, Jenny. You are almost family now. You could have the groom's flat above the garages; it is all newly refurbished and has great views."

Jenny nodded, pleased that there was no pressure from either of them to make a decision.

"It's a wonderful offer, Adrian, and I am really flattered and thrilled that you think I might be of use to you both. I promise I will think very carefully about it and give you my answer as soon as I possibly can."

"Fantastic," said Adrian; "tomorrow morning will be just fine!" He grinned, knowing perfectly well that Jenny would know he was teasing. "Who's for another glass of wine? I think we've earned it!"

Chapter Forty-One

Ask a Bright Horse

The night sky was inky black, but there was a glorious full moon and its light was so bright that it lit up the farm almost as if it were daytime. Moonbeams streamed through Jenny's bedroom window and, pretty as they were, they did nothing to help her get to sleep. Thoughts tumbled around in her head like children in a playground. She went over in her mind the hard work of the previous week, the events of the day, Tina's pleasure at how well she had done, the offer Tina had made her and Adrian's encouragement and obvious approval.

Only a year earlier, she had not known Daisy, Tina or Adrian, she had barely been able to sit on a horse, and now she had an amazing offer of a job she just knew she would love, and to become Daisy's owner as well was like a dream come true.

So much had happened in such a relatively short time and all for the better. She loved her life, relished each day and truly valued the affection and friendship she had found at the farm. Only a few months earlier, she would not have believed such happiness was possible. She would hate to make the wrong decision, hate to disappoint them. Could she really take on such a responsibility? What if she made a mess of it? There would be no second chances, she knew that. 'When in doubt, don't,' her mother used to say. The trouble was, if Jenny had followed that advice she would have achieved very little in her entire life, and in fact she would not even have learned to ride!

The ticking of the little clock in the bedroom seemed twice as loud as usual and sleep just would not come. She had been tossing and turning for several hours before she decided that a mug of hot chocolate might help to soothe and settle her down. She quietly rose and pulled a sweater over her nightdress, slipped out of the bedroom in her bare feet and quietly crept downstairs. It was warm in the kitchen. One of the dogs lifted its head and wagged its tail, the other continued to snore. Jenny grinned. *Great guard dogs*, she thought to herself. She sat on the old sofa slowly sipping her chocolate and thinking, wondering what the best thing to do was. The view from the kitchen window was bathed in moonlight and everything looked very calm and peaceful.

Jenny had a sudden urge to see Daisy; she had not been able to spend much time with her over the previous few days and had really missed her company. Once Jenny had finished her hot chocolate, she carefully let herself out of the kitchen door and selected a pair of wellingtons from the cheese room before going out into the garden. It was colder than she had imagined it would be and she drew the sweater tightly around herself. The yard was flooded with the light of the moon and it was very easy to see where she was going.

As she turned the corner towards the wooden yard she stepped into moon shadow, but the dark shadows held no threat and she wasn't afraid to be walking around in the middle of the night alone. Daisy was nowhere in sight as Jenny approached her stable, and she peeped over the door, not wanting to startle her. Daisy turned instantly and gave her the familiar nicker she had always used.

Jenny wondered if Daisy always slept so lightly, or perhaps, like her, Daisy couldn't sleep because of the full moon! The stable was dark and it took a moment for Jenny's eyes to attune to the gloom – she could only just make out Daisy's shape. She opened the door and slipped inside.

"Hi, girly!" she whispered. "I've come to ask your advice." Daisy turned towards her and came over to the door to put her head out and look around. She brought it back in again and turned to Jenny, her nose searching for Jenny's hands.

"I've nothing tasty for you, I'm afraid, poppet," Jenny said to her as she cupped Daisy's warm rose-pink velvet muzzle in her hands and slowly stroked her long nose repeatedly with her fingers. She could feel the warmth from Daisy's body as she stood next to her – it was comforting.

"You see, the thing is, Daisy," Jenny continued softly, "Tina wants me to come and live here all the time, she wants me to work for her. She says that if I come she will give you to me and you will be mine, all mine, forever, Daisy! I would be able to see you every single day, we would be together for always and no-one could take you away from me ever again. So, what do you think, Daisy? Would you like that? Do you think it's a good idea? Shall I tell Tina yes?"

Daisy slowly removed her nose from Jenny's hands, raised her head to look directly at Jenny and nodded, several times, most enthusiastically.

Jenny's face broke into a broad grin and she beamed with pleasure as she ruffled Daisy's forelock. "Then I will," she said as she put her arms around Daisy's neck and gave her a very long, very big hug.

"Thank you, Daisy," she said. "Do you know, instead of sharing one of your favourite cereal bars tomorrow, I think we should have one each to celebrate. Does that sound like a good idea as well?" And Jenny burst out laughing as Daisy lifted her head up and parted her lips.

GLOSSARY

BAY – a dark brown horse

BIT – a metal or synthetic bar which sits in the horse's mouth underneath its tongue

BLOCKS – coloured plastic blocks, used to rest poles upon to create a jump

BOX REST – when a horse is confined to its stable because of illness or injury

BUCK – the movement of a horse where it either kicks its back legs up in the air simultaneously or jumps off the ground with all four feet in the air at the same time

BUCKLE – the centre of the rein which fastens two halves of the rein together

CHESTNUT –a horse which is a ginger colour

CHURNED UP –when the grass in a paddock is ploughed up by the horses' feet in wet weather

CHANGE DIAGONAL – when a horse changes which

pair of legs it is leading with for a certain type of movement (gait), for example canter

CHANGE LEGS – when a horse changes which legs it is leading with

CHANGE THE REIN – to alter direction and encourage the horse to change its leading leg

CLEAN THEIR FEET –to clean the mud and stones out of a horse's hooves with a hoof pick

EXERCISE SHEET –a type of coat which a horse wears during exercise to keep its back warm

FETLOCK – the projection on the back of a horse's leg, just above and behind the hoof

FORELEG – the front leg of a horse

FORELOCK – hair which lies between the ears of a horse

GIRTH – a strap under the horse's tummy which fastens to the saddle on either side

GREEN UNDER SADDLE – an inexperienced horse which has not been ridden very much

HACK – a ride away from the stable, usually around the countryside

HANDS – a 10-cm measurement used to classify horses, e.g. 15 hands = 150 cm at the wither

HIND LEG – the back leg of a horse

LOOSEN GIRTH – the girth is loosened when the rider has dismounted and the horse is resting

MAIN YARD – the centre of a riding stable, usually where riders mount and rides begin

MANE – the hair over a horse's neck

NICKER/NICKERED – the soft low sound a horse makes in recognition or greeting

OPENED HER REIN – to move one rein away from the horse's neck to indicate direction

RUGS – a type of fabric coat which a horse may wear to keep it warm and dry

SADDLECLOTH – a padded fabric mat which lies on the horse's back underneath the saddle

SKIP OUT –to remove the droppings from either a paddock or a stable

SKIP TO CHANGE LEGS – a quick movement when a horse freely changes its leading legs

STABLE – a small building, usually of either brick or wood, which the horse lives in

STAND TO ONE SIDE – a groom stands at right angles to the horse, facing the horse's tail

TACK – any item a horse might wear, such as reins, saddle, bridle

TACK BOX – a box for keeping grooming items such as a brush or hoof pick

TIGHTEN GIRTH – to tighten the buckles which attach the girth to the saddle

TROTTING POLE – a wooden pole which is placed on the ground for a horse to trot over

WITHERS – the ridge between the shoulder blades of a horse